KU-676-968

Blood on the Sky

Will Hopkirk was all set to live the rest of his life with Diaglito's White Mountain Apaches, along with Sonseray, the beautiful Apache woman he married. But Diaglito was devastated when Tobias Hatch cold-bloodedly killed his twelve-year-old son, Choate. Nevertheless, Hopkirk persuaded the war chief to use the white man's court to give him justice.

Diaglito was humiliated and outraged when a not guilty verdict was brought in and vowed that only the spilling of white man's blood would satisfy the terrible wrong done to him and his people.

Now Hopkirk was forced to choose where his loyalties lay as the frontier erupted into a rage of violence.

Blood on the Sky

ELLIOT LONG

A Black Horse Western

ROBERT HALE · LONDON

© Elliot Long 2008
First published in Great Britain 2008

ISBN 978-0-7090-8636-9

Robert Hale Limited
Clerkenwell House
Clerkenwell Green
London EC1R 0HT

www.halebooks.com

The right of Elliot Long to be identified as
author of this work has been asserted by him
in accordance with the Copyright, Designs and
Patents Act 1988

DONCASTER LIBRARY & INFORMATION SERVICE	
30122031380682	
Bertrams	12/09/2008
W	£12.25

Typeset by
Derek Doyle & Associates, Shaw Heath
Printed and bound in Great Britain by
CPI Antony Rowe, Chippenham, Wiltshire

For my good friend
Paul Davey

THE KILLING

CHAPTER ONE

Arizona Territory, May 1888

Twelve-year-old Choate was feeling nervous. Something wasn't right. He could not put his finger on what it was, but it was there.

He eased his piebald pony to a stop. Through a gap in the tall pines rising above the aspen and sycamore-clothed slope he stared at the black mountains.

Their dark summits were still streaked with drift snow. They rose above the gnarled, stunted pines that signalled the end of the growth line up there. As far as he could make out there was nothing unusual going on. Nevertheless, this feeling of danger persisted. If anything, it was getting worse.

Feeling disgusted with his nervousness Choate sent his pony down-trail again; toward the level country Fort Nathan was situated on. He was being silly, a woman! There was nothing to be nervous about. His father, the White Mountain Apache war chief, Diaglito, made the treaty way back in 1882 with Grey Wolf, General George Crook, never to attack the white man again. In exchange, Grey Wolf promised – if the peace was not broken – his father and his people could live in their mountain home-land unmolested.

And Grey Wolf, unlike most white men, kept his word. It was Geronimo who was the troublemaker. But Geronimo and his followers were now at Fort Marion, Florida, prisoners of the white man. They were sent there two years ago, after surrendering to pony soldier chief Big Nose Captain, Lieutenant Charles Gatewood, deep in the Sierra Madres.

Choate frowned. So, why was he so edgy? Things were quiet now and he was nearly a man. He could take care of himself. In any case, his trip was inno-cent. He was on his way to Fort Nathan to trade furs for trinkets to give to his mother, and to continue to be taught to speak the white-man's tongue and learn to count the white-man's numbers by the fort doctor, Harland Spires.

That was what his father wanted him to do. His father emphasized it would be good for the son of Diaglito to learn the ways of the white man. If he learnt well, his father went on, the white man would not be able to cheat the White Mountain Apache any longer and things could only get better between the two peoples.

A blackbird called: *pip, pip, pip; pip, pip, pip,* its warning fading into the distance as the dark winged one went deeper into the trees.

Made uneasy once more, Choate let his gaze search the brush trailside and then the trees beyond. Still nothing. What was the matter with him? However, something must have disturbed the feathered one but there was no evidence as to what that might be. Maybe there was a hawk overhead?

Choate returned his thoughts to where he left them and recalled his pride when his father placed such faith in him. And he was quick to respond to his father's wishes. He buckled down, immersed himself in his studies, even though it was sometimes hard because he was used to roaming the mountains, hunting and tracking with his father, learning the ways of the Old Ones. Nevertheless, when he did arrive at Fort Nathan, he found the bustle of the place exhilarating and the white man fascinating, even though, at one time, his mother used to frighten him with tales about the white man and his cruelties, used to warn him they were demons and when he became a warrior he should go out and kill them all.

But that was a long time ago. Indeed, after his father made his peace with Grey Wolf, ten warriors of the tribe volunteered to scout for the pony soldiers. Then, five summers ago, Will Hopkirk, a former pony soldier chief, came to live amongst his father's people. Six months later a big feast was made and his father mingled blood with Hopkirk and made him his blood brother, proclaiming that white man and red man could live together in peace if the will was there.

Three weeks after that Hopkirk tied fifteen fine horses before Diaglito's wickiup and proclaimed he came to seek the hand of Sonseray and would not go away until he got it.

Sonseray, as everybody knew, was his father's ward. His father protected and looked after Sonseray and her mother, Star Child, after his friend Zele was killed by the white pony soldiers when White Mountain warriors were fighting Grey Wolf.

After the marriage ceremony Choate decided it would be right to call Hopkirk uncle because he always looked upon Sonseray as his aunt and Hopkirk said that was fine with him. He even said he was honoured to have Choate, the son of Diaglito, call him uncle. On the first day of going to learn the white man's tongue and numbers at Fort Nathan – which Hopkirk arranged with his army friend pony soldier chief Major John Dunstan – his uncle went along with him to introduce him to Doctor Harland Spires.

After the visit to the doctor's quarters, his uncle walked with him across the large parade ground and up the two steps to the low, lime-washed adobe building that overlooked the well-worn square. Part of the adobe building, Choate discovered on arrival, was pony soldier chief John Dunstan's office.

The major rose from his chair behind the scarred desk when they entered and came towards them. He looked at Hopkirk.

'Does he understand English, Will?' he said.

'A few words.'

Pony soldier chief Dunstan said, 'So, you want to learn the white-man's tongue, Choate?'

'Yes.'

Choate was surprised when Major Dunstan smiled, took his hand and shook it and said, '*Bueno.* Welcome to Fort Nathan. If you work hard you will find you will benefit greatly from your efforts.'

'My father has said it,' Choate said.

Now fascinated that the big pony soldier chief should treat him so well, Choate's gaze took in Major John Dunstan more fully. He was a tall, imposing man with ginger sideburns and a long auburn moustache that curled around the edges of his generous mouth. His hair was also ginger and was streaked with grey but thinning on the top. Choate thought he looked very fierce and decided that in the white man's world he must be a great warrior.

His uncle later said that this was true. Many years ago he and Major Dunstan fought many fierce battles together against their own tribe in the Land Where the Sun Rises. Hopkirk called it a Civil War. When the bloodshed ended, his uncle went on, they were sent out here to the land of the Apache to help quell the rebellious war chiefs who were causing trouble at that time: warriors such as Mangas Colorado, Victorio, Delshay, Chato and Cochise.

Then came the time, his uncle related, for him to re-enlist with the army. But instead, he went north to hunt buffalo and scout for the army up there. At that time the white man was at war with the Dakota Sioux and Northern Cheyenne. But when the Sioux war chief Crazy Horse was killed and Sitting Bull went to the Land of the Grandmother (Canada) the Sioux and Cheyenne made their peace. Hopkirk said it was then he got the urge to come back to the lands of the Apache.

'On my return,' he went on, 'Major John Dunstan greeted me warmly and introduced me to Grey Wolf. I already knew him. I scouted for him when he was fighting the Sioux and Northern Cheyenne. Up there they called him Grey Fox.' Hopkirk smiled. 'Grey Wolf seemed pleased to see me when I returned and he asked me to scout for him here. He suggested I could help recruit Apache scouts because I understood the language. It was while I was doing this I met your auntie, Sonseray. Soon, I wanted her to be in my wickiup and—'

The memory of his uncle's story snapped off, like

a light going out. This time there was a definite rustling in the bushes, the snort of a horse.

Choate closed his hand over the haft of his belt knife, his only weapon. He peered into the screen of trees. He relaxed when he saw it was the one his people called High Hat coming towards him through the greenery.

High Hat was slim, blond-haired and quick-eyed. One time High Hat also scouted for Grey Wolf when Geronimo and his renegades were making their trouble. Now High Hat hunted wolves and cougars for the white ranchers. Choate also heard High Hat tracked down badmen and took them to the law office in Nathan City, usually dead, so he could claim the reward money for their capture. It was also rumoured High Hat scalped Mexican *campasinos* and sold their hair back to the Mexican authorities as Apache scalps.

Choate saw High Hat was smiling at him, but he was always smiling and exposing his big yellow teeth.

High Hat held his Winchester carbine across his chest, as in the way of the Apache. As he came close he said, 'Well, howdy, boy?'

Choate was always pleased to have the opportunity to practise his English. 'The day goes well for you, Mr Hatch?'

He said 'Mr Hatch' because Dr Spires said it was correct for a boy to address a man in that way.

High Hat nodded, still grinning and said heartily,

'It sure does, boy.' Then he faded his smile and crinkled his face in an inquisitive manner. 'I guess you're on the way to Fort Nathan, uh?'

'Yes,' Choate said, 'I go to learn the white man's talk and learn how to count the white-man's numbers.'

High Hat said, 'Yeah, so I heard.'

'It is good for me, uh, Mr Hatch?'

High Hat pursed his lips as if he held some doubt about that. 'Well, I guess it all depends on which way you look at it,' he said.

High Hat now indicated with a dirty finger to the pelts Choate held draped across the withers of his frisky piebald pony; the furs he intended to trade for trinkets to give to his mother when he returned to the village.

'Seems you've been doing some hunting, boy,' he said.

Choate pushed out his chest 'Yes. I hunt well. My father taught me.'

'That'll be Diaglito, right?'

'Yes.' Choate looked keenly at High Hat. 'Do you know my father?'

High Hat said, raising sandy eyebrows, 'One mean Apache, I got to say.'

High Hat now waved a hand at the knife in the deerskin sheath, attached to the belt round the boy's waist. Choate still kept his hand resting upon the haft.

16

'That the knife you used to skin off those pelts, boy?'

'Yes.'

'It's a mighty handsome blade,' High Hat said. 'You didn't steal it, did you?'

Choate shook his head. 'There was no need to steal,' he said. 'Will Hopkirk, my uncle, gave it to me.'

'Uncle, uh?'

'Yes.'

High Hat reached out with a grubby hand. 'Mind if I take a look at it, boy? I mean, a man don't get to see a cutter like that every day of the week, now do he?'

'It is a Green River knife,' Choate said pushing out his chest. 'My uncle says it is the best there is.'

Hatch nodded and said airily, 'Well, he could be right at that.'

Choate eased the blade out of its belt sheath. He was about to turn it to present it haft first as Dr Spires taught him it was polite to do when High Hat said, 'Hell, no need for the fineries, boy; no need at all,' and swung his carbine around, pointed it and fired.

Choate felt a massive impact hit the centre of his chest. He gasped as the force of it drove all breath out of him and rammed him back. Strangely, he was more bewildered than frightened and he hardly heeded the birds that screamed their alarm calls as

17

they flew further into the trees.

Another detonation quickly followed. Choate felt another tremendous blow smash into his chest. The impact of this one knocked him out of his blanket saddle. He now realized the power in him was draining fast and he knew he must do something to defend himself. As in the manner of Diaglito he yelled his war cry and closed his hand around the haft of the knife and tried to get up. But a great tiredness was seeping into him.

Lying in the dust of the trail he stared into the cobalt blue of the morning sky; then at the sun's early morning rays flickering through the trailside trees dazzling his eyes. He became aware of a slow vast darkness creeping in from the edges of his vision.

After that he knew no more.

CHAPTER TWO

Tobias Marcellus Hatch rolled his tobacco quid across his wide mouth and pouched it to form a bulge in his hollow left cheek. He spat brown juice to the rocky ground and looked on dispassionately as Choate died. The boy's black eyes were wide open and staring into the bright spring morning.

After moments, Hatch slid his Winchester carbine into its saddle scabbard and wiped away the trickle of brown spittle that was rolling down the blond stubble on his weak chin. The echoes of his shots were dying away into the mountains. After moments a vast silence settled over the area.

Such silences did not bother him, he was used to them, and he was utterly indifferent to the murder he had just committed. Business was business. He was being paid $500 to do a job. Now it was done and that was the end of it.

What was one Apache brat, anyway? And who was to know he had done it . . . only the people who paid him handsomely for his services? And they wouldn't talk, he was cast-iron sure of that.

They were wealthy and influential people from Nathan City and beyond. They said they badly needed the Apache wars to start up again. The reason? They were losing money hand over fist because of the peace that now existed in the territory and it could not be allowed to go on.

Hatch grinned. Well, killing Diaglito's eldest son would, sure as hell, get things off to a rip-roaring start; get the red bastards butchering and looting and generally causing mayhem on a large scale. And, dammit, decided Hatch, he would sure go along with all of that.

Forts were closing down right left and centre. Trade in cattle, guns and God knew what else was almost at a standstill. Making an honest buck these days was a mighty hard thing to do in this territory. Why shouldn't the red bastards be fired up to start warring again?

Hatch let out a guffaw, but the noise from behind soon choked it off and sent his hand speeding for his handgun. However, the clicks of a gun being armed halted the drive.

'Raise your hands, you murdering scum!' rasped the voice from behind.

Frozen mid-action, Hatch felt his stomach congeal into an icy lump. At this early hour he thought he would be alone in the mountains, apart from the boy. Nevertheless, he put on his best grin and raised his arms and kneed his strawberry roan gelding around and stared at the tall, lean man with the thick, black moustache and hard grey eyes. Those narrow orbs seemed to eat right into him, as if striving to reach his soul. Hatch also noticed the man was aiming a Smith & Wesson Schofield six-shooter directly at his heart. Worst of all a shiny Deputy US Marshal's badge was pinned to the lapel of the man's worsted black coat.

But still grinning he said, 'Out kind of early, ain't you, Marshal? What's the matter, can't you sleep?'

The federal law representative met his stare with that steely, penetrating gaze. He was clearly without humour. 'Your flippancy is misplaced on these ears, mister,' he said. He lifted his chin. 'Now, to make things perfectly clear between us, I am Deputy US Marshal Hugh Mayer and though I do not feel inclined to explain anything to the likes of you, I will.

'I rise early when on the trail and right now I am riding to pick up a miscreant in Nathan City. Which is fortunate for, had I not been so doing, I would not have seen murder done here and would not have been able to apprehend the culprit.'

Hatch narrowed his eyelids and slowly spat brown tobacco juice into the dust. What the hell. . . ? *Miscreant? Apprehend? Culprit?* What kind of damned dude talk is that? Still grinning he said, 'Is that a fact now?' He screwed up his eyelids to express his curiosity. 'Just where d'you hail from, mister?'

'That is no concern of yours at this time.'

East was Hatch's guess. For the first time he melted his smile and formed his lips into a sneer. 'Now, just how in the hell do you figure I murdered that red squirt?' he said. Mayer half-turned in the saddle and pointed to a thick clump of brush, fifty yards back up the trail. 'I was right there, about to catch up, when you did it.' The lawman's tanned face set into grim lines. 'By God, mister, my hope is Nathan City's hangman is a novice and does not break your neck cleanly on the drop, so you will die slow and in great pain when we get you on that scaffold they're going to build for you there.'

Hatch decided there and then he did not like this asshole one little bit. He said, 'Why you smart-talking bastard, what makes you think—?'

With startling swiftness Mayer urged his chestnut mare forward with swift kicks. In an instant he was close enough to swing down his Schofield six-shooter and Hatch gave out a harsh cry when the long barrel impacted against his left cheekbone. Not content with that, the son of a bitch cut back to smash the barrel across the right side of his jaw. Hatch felt warm blood begin to run down his face and chin.

Meantime he heard Mayer's cold comment, 'No man besmirches my mother's good name with that

22

word, d'you hear me?'

Besmirches? What damn word?

Wrath poured through Hatch. His natural impetuosity drove his hand toward his Colt. But he didn't get even close. The cold steel of the business end of Mayer's Schofield pressed hard against his left temple.

'Go ahead, friend,' Mayer said.

Hatch swallowed on a throat that was now as dry as the Sonora desert. He raised his arms quickly as the muzzle of the Schofield pressed harder against his skull.

'Now, mister,' the marshal said, 'hand over your rifle and your Colt and do it very carefully.'

Hatch did so with great reluctance.

'The gun in the shoulder holster now,' Mayer said.

Extreme anger now filled Hatch . . . his ace in the hole? He was betting on that short-barrelled Colt Sheriff hidden there to get him out of this when the opportunity arrived. Once more impulse to do something grabbed him, but he swamped it. He wouldn't stand a chance against this man. Very carefully he eased the guns out of leather and passed them over. Mayer promptly tossed the lot into the bushes. Hatch glared. 'Damn you, they cost me a hundred bucks!'

Mayer said, 'You were robbed.'

'The hell I was!' Hatch said.

Mayer waved the Schofield. 'Climb down and put that Indian boy on his pony and fasten him down.'

New dissension flared through Hatch and he said, 'Mister, you can go to hell.' Dammit, it was like being asked to polish some damned black fellow's boots, for God's sake.

In reply, the bullet from Mayer's Schofield snatched the top hat clean off Hatch's head. Worse, the boom of the weapon in his ear set his head ringing. So much so he could barely hear Mayer's harsh demand, 'Get it done, damn you!'

Grinning his hate now, Hatch climbed down, picked up his hat and studiously poked his finger through the holes in it. Then he put it back over his matted and dirty blond hair. Next he lifted Choate's small, lifeless form and placed it over his pony and tied it down.

He stared up at the tall federal marshal.

'Now what?'

Mayer waved the Schofield. 'Get back on your horse, gather the hackamore on the boy's pony. We head for Nathan City.'

Still grinning, Hatch climbed up, stiffly and reluctantly. Seated in his range saddle he spat a stream of brown tobacco juice, which narrowly missed Mayer's left boot. Then he said, 'You got to think again on this, mister. That brat was about to put a knife in me.' He pointed with a long, dirty finger at the blade gripped in Choate's dead hand. 'See, he's

24

still got the damned cutter in his hand. Now in this part of the world that's evidence, mister, and you'd better believe it and cut out this crap and let me be on my way in peace.'

'You're an animal,' Mayer said. 'The only place for you is the gallows.'

Hatch grinned again, with some confidence. Soon this asshole was going to find out just how things worked around here. 'Is that a fact?' he said.

Guffawing he jerked at the rawhide rein looped around the muzzle of Choate's pony and spurred his roan down-trail toward Nathan City.

'Reckon you're about to get some education, mister,' he said.

CHAPTER THREE

By noon four days on Nathan City was buzzing. Folks were coming in from far and near to be here for the trial. Buggies, wagons and horses choked the town and the air was alive with speculation. For it was almost unknown around here to have a white man put on trial for killing some Apache brat. But, dammit, it was happening, like it or not.

And most didn't like it. The majority thought Apaches were no better than scum and better off dead so civilization could really come to this territory and make it fit for clean-living white folk to cultivate or run their cows on. And, dammit, there were valuable ores in those mountains just begging to be exploited.

And the town being full, extra barmen were hired and the four *cantinas* were doing roaring business. Every drinking place was a throb of boozy talk. In the Easy Rest saloon one fellow was buying and he was being distinctly forthright in his opinions about the present situation.

What was more, money from certain quarters was in his pocket, put there just to stir up feelings about the wrongness of Hatch's impending trial.

'So Hatch killed some damn White Mountain buck?' he was saying. He was standing on the pine stool surveying the sea of sweating faces around him, which were etched in the yellow light of the *cantina* lamps. 'So what?' he demanded. 'It isn't a cause to hang him. Hell, that damned Apache brat pulled a knife on Hatch, didn't he? Every man has a right to defend himself, hasn't he? Stands to reason.'

Fervent agreement buzzed around the gathered crowd.

'Dammit, boys,' the speaker went on, while grabbing his coat lapel in his right hand and looking important, 'them Apache bastards are in the hills right now, killing and looting. Hell, they're like rabid wolves and should be treated as such. Why, only last week two of the Mendoza family were butchered jest for the mule they were riding home on. Dammit, gents, it can't go on. Truth be known, we should be patting Hatch on the back and buying him drinks for killing that red son of a bitch, not threatening to put a rope around his neck! It's the old saying: nits make lice!'

'Damned right,' said a man nearby. He took a swig of beer and looked for agreement amongst the sweat-stinking men gathered around him and got it. He went on, 'Why, that government marshal should've minded his own Goddamned business and rode on. Am I right?'

'Right as hell,' voiced another.

'From East, ain't he?' demanded someone else. 'Dammit, what does he know about how things get done in these parts?'

'My sentiments exactly,' the first speaker said.

He let go of his lapel and lifted his index finger and waggled it, his voice vibrating with the feeling he put into his next words. 'Why, I tell you, boys, there'll be no peace in this land until every one of those red scum are dead. Every right-thinking man in this territory knows this to be a certain fact.'

Another of the crowd said, 'It should never have come to court. What in tarnation is Sheriff Carmody thinking about – going along with that federal marshal's hogwash?'

'He didn't *go along*,' said the man beside him. 'Carmody told me he only humoured the man and not to worry about it. At the end of the day it would-n't amount to a hill of beans what that damned marshal thinks, or says. Influential people around here have got Hatch the best lawyer available.' The fellow hitched up his gunbelt and nodded his bearded head. 'Boys, I tell you right now: Hatch won't be in that dock more'n five minutes.'

'How d'you know?' said another.

'I got that on the best authority, that's how,' said the Beard.

'Even so,' said a worried-looking man standing with them and known for his liberal views, 'it's not Diaglito's band that was doing the killing around here and that was his boy Hatch killed. Dammit, let's be fair about this, boys, those White Mountain braves scouted for the army for God knows how long. Why, they led Lieutenant Gatewood to Geronimo's hideout.' The fellow shook his head. 'Gents, I'm concerned about this. Do we really want to go back to the old days of killing and looting, having our women scared out of their wits and being raped and murdered, our children kidnapped, or just plain butchered?' He looked around him. 'Diaglito's in town right now; he's come in to see white-man's justice done for his boy. By God, gents, if we don't get this right there could be the devil to pay.'

'And "right" meaning what?' said a man nearby.

'Meaning Hatch murdered that boy according to that federal marshal and should be hanged for it. We should show Diaglito the white-man's justice is good for him as well as us.'

'He talking crazy,' roared a burly fellow at the back. 'Dammit, somebody get hold of the yellow bastard and throw him out. Hanging a man for killing some damned Apache? It's never been heard of!'

A chorus of agreement went up and the fellow went white-faced when he was roughly grabbed and lifted high and carried struggling the length of the *cantina*. At the open doors he was hurled into the dust and horseshit.

Hitting the ground amongst the row of horses at the tie rails, the man back-pedalled on all fours, straining to avoid being kicked by the milling hoofs. Once clear of the beasts he picked himself up and dusted himself down and stared at the crowd gathered outside the saloon doors, jeering at him and waving their arms. He set his face once more into determined lines.

'Boys, listen to me,' he called, 'that court has got to find Hatch guilty and hang him for what he's done.'

One drunken cowboy yelled, 'Dammit, don't he ever learn?'

He drew his Colt .45. Soon lead was exploding fountains of dust around the unarmed objector's boots. When lead ripped the heel off his left boot the fellow made a hasty retreat down the sun-seared street.

Guffawing and backslapping, the crowd went back into the dim recesses of the packed saloon. Now, drink in hand, the original speaker took up a position at the bar. He finished his whiskey and pulled a large watch out of his vest pocket. After studying it he looked up and said, 'Better be moving, boys, the trial starts in ten minutes. Judge Frank Cain is residing and he don't like interruptions once he gits going.'

Clearly not wanting to miss a trick, the crowd, whooping and cheering, surged out of the *cantina*. On the street they moved toward the recently built clapboard courthouse on the northern edge of town.

To add to the din they drunkenly boomed Colt lead into the pale-blue sky, filling the air with acrid gunsmoke. Soon, bunches of men from the other *cantinas* – equally as strident and inebriated – were piling out on to the street and joining them. One fellow whooped a Rebel cry then yelled, 'By God, boys, there going to be a high time in the old town tonight, after Hatch gets his freedom! And that son of a bitch Indian, Diaglito, better get his ass out of town or he'll be next!'

More yeeehaaahs ripped the air; more guns exploded.

CHAPTER FOUR

Will Hopkirk was sitting atop his roan gelding at the head of Nathan City's main drag. The town was now fifteen years old – as old as Fort Nathan. It sprawled haphazardly before him. Little planning had gone into it. Bits were added on as and when it was needed, and the smell that pervaded the place suggested the sanitary facilities had not kept up with the expansion.

Hopkirk gazed at the clapboard façade of the courthouse. Beside him his blood brother was sitting motionless atop his pinto pony, also staring. Diaglito was a squat, deep-chested White Mountain Apache war chief. His jet-black eyes glittered in sunken sockets. His thin lips formed a cruel gash under his hooked nose. He was wearing a charcoal-dark white man's suit. Atop his head, set precisely, was a black beehive hat. An eagle feather was stuck at an angle in the hatband. He looked distinctly uncomfortable in the outfit.

Hopkirk met the chief's intent gaze when it turned to him. 'I have changed mind, my brother,' Diaglito said in Apache. 'The white-man's court is no good for Apache. We should have catched the killer of Choate ourselves and tried him the Apache way. I am feeling Apache way would be much better than white man's.'

'We agreed to give this a chance, Diaglito,' Hopkirk said. 'At least the US marshal brought High Hat in.'

'Sure,' said the war chief, 'but even Hopkirk knows in his heart this will not work; that there will be no justice for the son of Diaglito here in Nathan City.'

'Better wait and see,' Hopkirk said.

Diaglito grunted and returned his gaze to the street. Hopkirk also stared at the crowds now emptying out of Nathan City's four saloons. He observed most were as drunk as skunks. He turned to Diaglito.

'We'd better get inside before the court fills up.'

Diaglito didn't answer, just nodded.

They dismounted, tied their horses to the nearest hitch rail and began to walk across the dusty street toward the courthouse.

Hopkirk was feeling distinctly uncomfortable. There were a large number of people gathered and they were all staring at Diaglito. It was not hard to read their thoughts: it wasn't every day of the week a man got to see a full blood Apache war chief close up and in Nathan City.

Of a sudden, somebody called, 'Figuring on getting some justice, Chief?'

Jeering guffaws went up.

'Not a hope in hell, I'd say,' yelled another. 'Huh, boys?'

More sneering comments came thick and fast.

Unease began to build up in Hopkirk. There was no accounting for what a mob would do once it got roused. Worse was to come. The voice that came to them from behind was quiet, purring and hate-filled. 'Diaglito, you son of a bitch, I've come to git your hide. But afore I do I want you to know that brat of yours got all he was due. My only concern is . . . he didn't suffer enough. If it had been left to me I'd have fried his balls over a hot fire afore I slit him from crotch to breastbone and let him die slow.'

Hopkirk felt Diaglito stiffen beside him. They both turned to see the fellow was a tall, range-lean cowman. He was standing about ten feet away. He was swaying drunkenly and an evil grin exposed his rotten, tobacco-stained teeth. He was holding a half-empty whiskey bottle in his left hand. Hopkirk doubted it was the first one of the day.

As the fellow moved close, Hopkirk could smell the drink and sweat and cow shit on him. His denim outfit was faded and patched and his grey Stetson hat was almost black around the bottom, no doubt made that way through years of wear and sweat. Worst of all, the man's right hand was posed over his Colt .45, which was housed in a worn holster on his left hip butt forward, in the manner of the Texas draw. The gunbelt around his waist was half filled with bright cartridges.

The fellow was staring specifically at Diaglito. He was saying, 'You're like Goddamned quicksilver. Five years I've waited for this chance. Why? Because you killed my partner, flayed him alive.' The man spat directly into Diaglito's face. 'Now,' he hissed, 'make your play, or die anyway.'

Diaglito flinched as the brown spittle struck. His face set as if made of granite chunks and his obsidian eyes glowed red. His hand started for the big Bowie knife in the belt around his middle but Hopkirk's hand restrained him. He said, in Apache, 'Is this true, my brother?'

Diaglito gravely shook his head. 'I know nothing of this thing. One Apache much like another to white man.'

Hopkirk nodded. 'That's good enough for me. Now, let me handle this because if you try anything this crowd with tear you apart in two seconds flat.'

He could see Diaglito was not happy with the situation. The war chief reached up and touched the spittle trickling down his left cheek. Then he took his hand away and examined the spittle curiously before he said, still using Apache, 'I have heard

your words, my brother, and I will go with them.'
Then he added, 'But do not kill this man. That pleasure must be Diaglito's.'

Hopkirk said, 'Perhaps what I do will be enough.'

Diaglito shook his head. 'My brother should not
rely on that.'

Hopkirk said, 'No.'

He turned to the 'puncher who was frowning at
him. 'Hell's going on?' he said.

Hopkirk met his stare. 'You will answer to me,
mister.'

The cowboy looked at the faces around him and
then took a fresh hold on the butt of his Colt. 'What
d'you mean: answer to you? Let the yellow bastard
fight his own battles, dammit. This ain't your business.'

'I'm making it mine,' Hopkirk said.

With suddenness he swung his right fist and
buried it in the puncher's whiskey-sodden face and
found pleasure in feeling his knuckles crunch
against bone and flesh.

The fellow yelled and staggered back, his arms
flailing and trying to keep his balance but he
sprawled on his ass into the dust and horseshit on
the street. With the impact, the bottle of whiskey
flew from his left hand and the Colt from his right.
Blood was running freely from his mashed nose.
Glowering up, the fellow spat out two rotten teeth
and shook his head. Evil glittered in his sky-blue

eyes. 'Why, you no good son of a bitch!' he breathed.

He scrambled to his feet and Hopkirk met him on the up and kicked him in the solar plexus.

The cowboy doubled over as air 'woofed' out of him. Hopkirk followed up without pity and again buried his thick-soled, knee-length, Apache moccasin boot into the puncher's flat gut. As the fellow went down, vomit jetted out of his mouth and splattered down his worn denim shirt and the chaps over his denim trousers.

The smell of the sick drifted up to Hopkirk's nostrils on the hot air. He was himself faintly nauseated by the stench.

The fellow lay for a while moaning, then he rolled over to get on to all fours and stared at the dust of the street under him. There he waited some more, shaking his head as if to clear it.

Hopkirk knew he should hold back; wait to see if there was any more fight left in the man. However, he was so outraged by the disgusting thing just done to Diaglito and for no good reason, he drew his Cavalry Colt and began beating the puncher about the head.

The fellow howled and attempted to fend off the swinging metal with his raised left arm, but Hopkirk continued until there was a sickening crack when the fellow's left ulna split apart. Screaming, the cowboy went down on his knees hugging the broken arm against his body.

Hopkirk stared down at him. He saw fragments of puke hanging from the bristles on the fellow's chin. The gash on his left cheekbone was running ripe blood. Another injury made a vivid incision along his chin, which was also running red. Top of that, gore was running from the fellow's shattered nose and from the two lacerations made in his scalp. Both his eyes were swelling up fast.

Hopkirk found himself willing the man to stay down. But the crazy bastard wouldn't. He slowly climbed to his feet and stood wiping blood from his mouth with a shaking hand. Then he mumbled through badly split lips, 'Mister, I'll kill you for this!' He lurched forward, his good fist flailing.

Hopkirk easily evaded his attack. Balanced, he smashed his right fist into the fellow's mouth. Then his roundhouse left hook crunched against the fellow's right ear and split it. The 'puncher's head snapped back. Blood and saliva sprayed from his mouth and he sank to the ground.

Hopkirk looked on without pity but thought: stay down, man, for God's sake. But the crazy bastard began climbing his feet. Once more he stood swaying and shaking his head. Both eyes were now about closed. Even so, he took another swing.

Hopkirk avoided it with ease and caught the man with a tremendous right, then a left and another right – pounding blows that split what little defence the man could put up. It was clear the fellow was near out on his feet. But Hopkirk kept swinging until he felt powerful arms pin his own to his sides and the voice in his ear say, 'For God's sake, Will, you'll kill him.'

The red fighting mists cleared. Hopkirk turned as best he could. It was Sergeant Pat Ryan of C Troop, Fort Nathan, who was clamping his arms to his sides. Many were the patrols he and Pat Ryan had ridden together into Apache territory when Crook was winkling Geronimo and his cutthroats out of their mountain strongholds. He let his anger die.

He said calmly, 'It's all right, Pat; you can let go.'

Ryan's grey gaze was searching. 'You sure now, bucko?'

'I'm sure.'

He felt the pressure of Ryan's grip gradually ease. When he was released he stared down at the blood-soaked puncher moaning on the ground and said, 'You've more guts than sense, mister.'

The fellow looked up, tried to focus his swollen gaze. 'I'll git you, mister, see if I don't.'

Incensed once more by the man's stupidity Hopkirk swung his right foot and smashed it into the fellow's exposed face.

'That wouldn't be a good idea,' he sad.

He turned to Diaglito, who was looking on impassively. 'Let us go, my brother,' he said in Apache.

39

Diaglito nodded, his stern face without expression. The hushed crowd parted. They were clearly in awe of the violence just witnessed. Hopkirk ignored their stares and with Diaglito by his side entered the near-filled courthouse.

CHAPTER FIVE

The air inside the building was stiflingly hot. Hopkirk found two unoccupied seats near the back of the hall and Diaglito and he sat down. Hopkirk observed Hatch was seated up front on the other side of the rails that separated the court from the ranks of benches provided for those who had come in to hear proceedings.

Hatch's head, Hopkirk noticed, was bandaged and his eyes were purple, bruised orbs above the plaster on his nose. He'd heard about the beating Hatch had taken from the federal marshal who arrested him. Nevertheless, despite his battered state, Hatch was clearly swaggeringly confident as to the outcome of the trial.

Cold anger settled upon Hopkirk. There was the man who had killed the boy he'd held in great affection, the boy who called him 'uncle', the boy who was – Hopkirk closed his eyes as the painful reminder of the murder hit him again – *had* been eager to learn the white-man's ways and customs. Choate was the

41

hope for the future, Hopkirk thought. Would sanity ever come to this tormented land?

Hopkirk opened his eyes. He saw Hatch was looking over his shoulder and grinning around at the full courtroom. He was waving to people he knew. Hopkirk found his arrogance nauseating.

It was at that moment Hatch spotted them. His grin spread even wider as he directed his gaze solely upon Diaglito. 'Come to see justice done, Chief?' he called, above the excited murmurings of the crowd. 'Kind of like me walking free; the court finding your boy brung it on himself?'

Guffaws came from the crowded courtroom.

Hopkirk felt Diaglito stiffen beside him. He gripped his arm. 'Ignore him,' he said. 'Let the court decide.'

Diaglito said, his dark stare fathomless, 'You think much of your law, my brother. I do not. But you asked me to use it and I have done so, even though my son is dead and my heart is broken.' He pointed towards Hatch. 'However, if it happens the carrion who is called High Hat is hanged, then I will see the white-man's law is good for the Apache and I will follow his path for ever. But if High Hat is freed. . . .'

Diaglito's last sentence sent chills coursing up Hopkirk's backbone. Its tone left him in no doubt as to what Diaglito meant by his menacing innuendo . . . war would once more decimate this territory, as sure as night followed day.

42

Circuit Judge Frank J Cain, a tall, skinny, sour-faced man with pince-nez perched on his beak of a nose, came bustling into court through a side door. He sat down behind his desk, sniffed and stared owlishly around the packed courtroom. He got right down to business. 'Is there a defence?'

The young local lawyer, Phil Collier, rose from his chair. 'Sir.'

'Prosecution?' said Cain.

'Deputy US Marshal Mayer, Judge,' said Sheriff Tom Carmody coming to his feet. Carmody was the elected law in the county.

Judge Cain stared at the tall, wide-shouldered, dour-looking federal lawman in the grey suit and black string tie, seated on the chair provided for him. Mayer, he saw, was preening his black, walrus moustache.

Judge Cain raised his thin brows, frowned and returned his gaze to Sheriff Carmody and said testily, 'Is there no practising lawyer?'

Carmody coughed and shuffled on scuffed-up size eleven boots. 'Diaglito said the federal officer would speak for him. He said he has read his heart and knows his words to be good.'

Some in the crowded courtroom sniggered. Judge Cain glared at them. When silence prevailed he said, 'Very well, let's get on with it. I've four more cases to hear yet and I got to be on the noon stage for Harkness Springs tomorrow.' He stared at

US Marshal Mayer.

'Will you start proceedings, Deputy?'

Mayer rose and told it the way he saw it. When he was finished Judge Cain frowned at him.

'Is that it?'

Mayer nodded. 'Yes, sir.' He pointed to Hatch. 'That man murdered the Indian boy without provocation. I have no doubts about it.'

Judge Cain raised thin brows in a slightly condescending way. 'Really. Well, that will have to be proved, Deputy.'

'I just did, sir,' Mayer said.

Judge Cain said, a slightly sardonic smile on his face, 'You will find things are not quite as simple as that in a court of law, Deputy Mayer.' He turned his owlish stare on to Collier. 'Defence? D'you want to question this officer?'

'Yes, sir.' Collier gazed at the US marshal. 'Deputy Mayer, where were you when you witnessed this alleged murder?'

'In the trees trailside, maybe fifty yards away,' Mayer said, 'and there was no alleged about it.'

A faint smile crossed Collier's lips. 'Yes, but as Judge Cain has pointed out, we need proof of that. Now, you say the deceased was handing a knife to my client?'

'Yes. It appeared to me that Hatch asked to see it.'

'*Appeared* to you, Deputy?' said Collier. He raised dark eyebrows and glanced at the jury before

44

returning to Mayer. 'But you didn't actually *hear* my client ask to see the weapon. Is that right?'

Mayer said, 'It would be plain to any man with a modicum of perception to see what was going on.'

'Would it indeed?' Collier said. He fumbled with some papers on the desk before him before adding, with a smug smile, 'May I explain, Marshal Mayer, that *would be* is not fact, and a court of law can deal only in facts.'

Mayer frowned, his grey gaze setting steel-hard under craggy brows. He said, 'Are you calling me a liar, sir?'

Collier held up his hands and shook his head. 'No, indeed not, Deputy Mayer; I'm sure you are telling us the truth the way you saw it. What I am saying – or trying to point out – is no two people ever see the same situation in the same way and that you perhaps misread what was actually occurring.'

Mayer snapped, 'Misread be damned. Hatch had some ulterior motive in mind when he asked to see that knife; I felt it in my gut. I think he wanted to get the weapon into the boy's hand to give him an excuse to murder him.'

Collier raised sandy brows and smiled again, looking at the jury before turning back to Mayer. 'Really, Deputy, now you are taking us into the realms of fantasy. What is this . . . ulterior motive . . . murder in mind . . . gut feeling? We need proof, sir, proper proof and not innuendo.'

Mayer scowled. 'You know what I mean, dammit.'

'Sadly, sir, I do not,' said Collier.

He tucked two fingers into his right vest pocket and began to walk thoughtfully across the floor. He stopped in front of the jury benches, then turned and faced the federal marshal.

'Deputy Mayer, according to my client, this is what actually took place. The Indian youth, Choate, pulled that knife on him. He was in no doubt the boy intended to kill him with it and—'

Mayer's hard-toned interruption cut the air across the courtroom. 'Hold on, mister, just now you were pulling me up about fantasizing. How did Hatch know what the boy intended if that weren't fantasizing?'

Collier smirked once more. 'Well put, sir. However, my client is a frontiersman and as everybody in these parts knows such men develop an instinct for these things. It's what keeps them alive. My client is convinced that, had he not used his rifle when he did, he would not be here today to tell the tale.'

Collier paused and waved his hand around the crowded courtroom. 'What is more, I feel it is safe to say there is not a man in this room who would not have done the same thing should he have been faced with a similar situation.'

Shouts of agreement chorused through the court. Judge Cain banged down his gavel. 'Silence!' he said, and turned to Collier. 'Counsellor, stop

46

playing to the crowd.' He turned to Marshal Mayer. 'Now, how do you reply, Deputy?'

Mayer looked around the courtroom, his gaze stern. 'I know what I saw.' He pointed a long finger at Hatch. 'That coward murdered the Indian boy and, by God, he should hang for it.'

Hatch came to his feet, clearly irate. 'Dammit, Judge, I don't have to listen to this!' Judge Cain wafted a hand. 'Sit down.' He turned his beady stare. 'Deputy Mayer, moderate your language.'

'Just telling the truth, Judge,' the federal marshal said.

'Truth has to be proved.' The judge focused on Collier. 'Counsellor?'

'Thank you, Judge,' Collier said. He turned, his face now grave and serious. 'Deputy Mayer, while you clearly believe what you saw was murder you still need to prove it, as the judge has pointed out. So far, this court has only heard hearsay – what you *think* you heard and what you *thought* you saw.'

Collier sighed and paused, as if searching for the right words before he said, 'No one here doubts your sincerity, Deputy Mayer, but – and I am sure Judge Cain will back me up on this – you have not placed sufficient evidence before this court to enable it to make a serious judgement on this. Furthermore, was there any need to beat up my client the way you did?'

'He insulted my mother by calling me a bastard,'

47

said Mayer. 'Now, I allow no man to do that. As for evidence: doesn't the word of a federal lawman stand for anything in this place?'

'Of course it does,' Judge Cain was quick to say, 'but, as Counsel has pointed out, we need *proof*, Deputy, and so far that proof has not been forthcoming.'

Mayer said, coolly, 'I know what I saw, Judge. Hatch killed that boy in cold blood. There's no doubt in my mind.'

'Yes,' Judge Cain said, 'but you have not *proved* that and that is what you must do.' He turned to Collier. 'Counsellor? Anything else?'

Collier got out of his seat and stared across the room to where the marshal was sitting. 'Deputy Mayer, though it is not the job of the defence to help the prosecution in any way, I feel it is incumbent upon me – due to your obvious lack of experience, and in the interests of justice – to suggest that if you could produce any other witness to the alleged crime this might help your submission.'

Deputy Mayer growled, 'Dammit, it was six o'clock in the morning, in the foothills of the mountains—'

'Maybe you should ask the birds, uh, Marshal?' called somebody from the crowded courtroom.

Hoots of laughter went up and the gavel banged down.

'Silence!'

The room rumbled into quiet and Judge Cain turned to Mayer. 'Well, Marshal? Are there any other witnesses?'

Mayer shook his head. 'None that I know of, sir.'

Judge Cain sighed, as if regretfully and prompted, 'Do you wish to cross-examine the accused?'

Mayer glared at Hatch. 'It'd be a waste of time. The man is an out and out liar.'

Hatch came to his feet with even more indignation. 'Dammit, Judge!'

Judge Cain said impatiently, 'Sit down!' He returned his attention to Mayer and said more gently, 'Deputy, let me remind you the accused is on oath and that he is obliged to tell the truth.'

Mayer said, 'It won't do no good. He is a disciple of the Devil. The sworn oath on the Bible will have no meaning to him.'

Hatch came up out of his seat once more. 'Hell's fire, Judge, you've got the truth from me. That red brat pulled a knife. I had no option but to kill him and that's the truth of it.'

Judge Cain sighed, wiped his sweaty brow, and lifted the desk lid before him and took a nip of whiskey from the flask hidden there and felt better. Dropping the lid he turned to Collier. 'Have you anything to add, Counsellor?'

Collier said, 'Only this, Judge.' He turned to the jury. 'My client is adamant he was approached and attacked with a knife by this Apache boy they call Choate and that he had no choice but to defend himself. Naturally, he deeply regrets the boy was killed, but at the time – as you no doubt will appreciate – he needed to act quickly. There is no more to it than that. It was self-defence and I ask you to deliver a verdict of not guilty.'

Judge Cain looked Mayer. 'Deputy, you anything to say?'

Mayer turned to the jury, his face set in grim lines. 'He's a killer, boys. You've got to hang him.'

Judge Cain said, 'Sadly, you have not proved that, Deputy.' He turned to the jury and added, 'Gentlemen, retire to make your decision. But don't take too long about it, I've another case to hear in ten minutes.'

The foreman came to his feet. He wore a huge grin. 'There's no need, Judge; Hatch's not guilty. Ain't no doubt about it.'

Whoops erupted from the full courtroom. Hats went into the air and men hugged each other and slapped each over on the back in pure delight. Judge Cain banged down his gavel. 'Silence, dammit!' he said and turned to Sheriff Carmody. 'Very well, release the prisoner. Bring in the next case soon as you're able.' Then he raised the lid of his desk and took another swig from his whiskey flask.

Diaglito came to his feet, his eyes glittering chips of obsidian. He walked out of the building looking neither right nor left. Hopkirk followed him, to defend the war chief's back on the ride out of town more than anything.

They fought their way through catcalls and hoots of derision and mounted stiffly and rode out of the now hostile town. At the fork in the trail three miles out, Hopkirk made to turn off for Fort Nathan. His intention was to report the court's decision to his friend Major John Dunstan. He knew – Dustan being a veteran of many Apache outbreaks – he would not receive it as good news.

Before they parted he said to the grave-faced Diaglito, 'You have been wronged, my brother, but do not do anything while your temper is hot. When you have cooled and considered this meet me tomorrow in the secret place we both know. We will find a way out of this, never fear.'

Diaglito's granite-like face set into severe lines before he said, 'I fear that way has gone, my brother.'

Hopkirk said, 'At least let us talk about it.'

'Talk. Always talk.' Diaglito let his words fade into the hot breeze. A long period of thoughtful silence passed before he spoke again. 'I will hear your words because you are my brother and I will respect them, but they will need to be powerful words.' With that he turned his horse around and headed across country. Hopkirk stared after him with serious eyes.

It didn't look good.

CHAPTER SIX

Nathan City the next day, minutes before dawn; José Ortega, the cleaner who worked for the Easy Rest saloon, was emptying a bucket of filthy mop water down the alley at the back of the building. Before returning to the barroom he stopped and stared at the prostrate figure against the saloon wall, almost hidden by the purple gloom.

José approached the vague outline cautiously. Maybe it was some drunk sleeping off last night's celebrations and would not appreciate being disturbed. Nevertheless, José bent to get a closer look, for there was something odd about the way the sleeper was lying.

And there was also the stench.

José was all too familiar with the smell of death. It was ever-present in this lawless land, where life was cheap and the law was thin on the ground. But when he saw who it was and the state he was in, José gasped and staggered back and made the sign of the cross before he threw up his breakfast of bean-filled tortillas.

The throat of Tobias Marcellus Hatch was cut from ear to ear. His eyes were gouged out and his stomach was slit from crotch to breastbone. To pile on the ghastliness of it the man's entrails were heaped across his boots and green horse dung was stuffed into the empty stomach cavity.

Gasping for breath, José staggered into the saloon. For moments he clung to the long walnut bar while he tried to gather his demeanour. When he did he went out through the swing doors and ran down Nathan City's main drag, shrieking out the news to anybody with ears to listen. Even so, it took time for the residents to stumble out on to the dawn-cool streets. It took even more time for them to rub sleep – induced by the previous night's overindulgence in rotgut – out of their puffy eyes before they got to asking what the hell all the noise as all about.

Sheriff Carmody was one of the first out and grabbed José. The cleaner babbled out his story, repeatedly making the sign of the cross across his narrow chest and wailing '*Madre de Dios*' in between.

When it became clear what José was going on about in his broken English, disbelief was on every face. After a pregnant pause, the crowd surged up the wheel-rutted street and rushed through the saloon doors and on into the back office, then out into the alley beyond.

In no time at all many of them were staggering away, puking up last night's supper. Sheriff Carmody appeared to be the only one to show little emotion as he stared down at the gruesome corpse. After a while, he said, to nobody in particular, 'By God, I've seen some bad things in my time, but this beats all.'

What was more he held few doubts as to who committed this awful atrocity: the White Mountain Apache war chief, Diaglito.

CHAPTER SEVEN

By mid-morning the sheriff's thirty-strong posse was dusting its way south, thinking to head off Diaglito before he crossed the border. Meanwhile, Hopkirk found the White Mountain war chief in the water-fed canyon they knew so well in the red rock country ten miles north of Nathan City.

Diaglito was sitting by the small bubbling stream before the tortured, naked body of the cowboy who had insulted him yesterday by spitting on him. The man was in a terrible state. Hopkirk could only work out who he was by recognizing his range garb, which was scattered around his body.

The fellow was still hanging head down over a small, now dead fire. A rope around his ankles was holding him suspended from the bough of the streamside cottonwood. The rope was creaking as the body swayed gently in the hot breeze moaning down the narrow canyon.

The sight was so horrible Hopkirk found difficulty in hanging on to his steak and fries breakfast eaten with Major Dunstan an hour earlier.

The fellow's skull was charred, his hair burnt off. His cooked eyes bulged and most of his facial flesh was baked, the skin cracked and curled to resemble flakes of burnt paper. The flesh beneath was the colour of roast pork. Top of that, the man's naked body was criss-crossed with shallow cuts.

Looking at the gashes Hopkirk decided it was reasonable to assume the knife, now cased in Diaglito's belt sheath, was the weapon that made those incisions. The blood from the wounds was dark and dry on the fellow's white torso. Gore also blackened the sandy ground below the body. Masses of flies were feasting off the blood. If the fellow had possessed a face, Hopkirk decided, the agony etched into it would have been indescribable.

He realized Diaglito was looking intently up at him from where he was sitting, on the canyon floor. The war chief said, 'Are you shocked, my brother?'

Hopkirk knew he shouldn't be. He was acquainted with Apache methods of torture, witnessed it second hand in burnt out homesteads and settlements on more than one occasion during his army service and civilian scouting years.

He said, 'It is not the way of my people, *mi hermano.*'

Diaglito smiled. 'You think so? Look again, my friend. Look at the things that have been done to

56

my people and the peoples of other nations by the white man. Travellers from the plains and other parts come to our lands occasionally – to trade, as well as to make war. They speak of terrible things: of land being stolen, of horse herds killed or scattered; of women and children butchered; women's genitals cut out and fastened to pony soldiers' saddle cantles as trophies. Winter food stocks burnt and villages razed to the ground and people, some naked, driven out into the winter storms to die in the bitter cold. And this happening when sometimes the white man's flag is flying over their tipis, to show their allegiance to the Great White Father in Washington. Is that conduct any better than what has happened here?'

Hopkirk said, 'Diaglito, this is not the same. Most of that was done in the heat of battle. This is calculated and—'

Diaglito raised his hand for silence. 'I think not, my brother,' he said. 'Years ago, the great Mimbreño war chief, Mangas Colorado, came into the white-man's camp to talk peace, but the pony soldiers tortured him with hot bayonets on his feet and legs when he was trying to get some sleep by their camp-fire. When he called them children and cursed them they shot him and scalped him and dumped his headless body in a ditch. He was seventy years old.'

Diaglito pointed at the mutilated corpse before

them. 'At least this is honest. It is as it says in the Book of the Black Robes* "an eye for an eye, a tooth for a tooth". But then I have heard there are many contradictions in your Book. In another part it says: "Thou shalt not kill".' Diaglito frowned. 'This does not make sense to me. Does it make sense to you?'

Hopkirk admitted silently that parts of the Bible would take some explaining and he wasn't about to start now, even if he could. Though he was never a religious man, during the Civil War, when things got real hot he did pray to God he would be spared.

He said, 'Did you kill High Hat?' News had come through to Fort Nathan an hour before he left.

Diaglito said, 'Could I have done otherwise?'

'You could have done it clean,' Hopkirk said, 'put a bullet through his brain, or a knife in his heart. You could have done the same with this poor wretch.' He waved a hand at the dead man.

Diaglito's fierce face was as though carved from granite; expressionless yet speaking volumes in its implacable determination. He said, 'That would have been too easy for them.'

'But more palatable to the white men who matter,' Hopkirk said; 'men of the Bureau for Indian Affairs; men I will have to deal with to try and explain this and give you a fighting chance to talk peace again.'

* Spanish Priests

Diaglito spat his contempt into the dust. 'Those men who are appointed to look after the Apache at San Carlos and elsewhere are coyotes; they are sly and greedy; always ready to sell the reservation Apache short. They deprive the Apache of decent food and clothing. They buy the cheapest beef, fit only for dogs; they buy rotting grain that makes my people sick so they can pocket the profit they make. They are leeches, my brother, living off my people's misery.'

'Some of them are good men,' Hopkirk said.

'And some are not.'

Diaglito rose from his cross-legged position. He dusted himself down and pointed to the east, beyond the mouth of the canyon. Hopkirk saw the range of mountains that Diaglito had made his homeland years ago. The canyon in which he and Sonseray had made their home was there, too. The mountains stood as purple bulks on the far horizon, huge, white-topped and majestic.

Diaglito said, 'When the sun rose over the mountains this morning, my brother, I saw much blood on the sky.'

Hopkirk felt his gut tighten. Such a phenomenon would usually mean rain was on the way to a white man. But to Diaglito . . . Hopkirk felt it reasonable to assume it told a very different story. It was a sign from their great God Yosen. The sign would speak to Diaglito of war, of bloodshed on a large scale – of the Apache rampaging across the land killing and looting and wreaking vengeance for the injustices done to the people to whom Yosen gave this land.

With some desperation, Hopkirk said, 'Think more on this, my brother. I will be the first to admit you have been badly wronged, but now the killer of Choate is dead and the one who spat on you is dead; justice has been served; the honour of your people satisfied. Let it be enough. Return to your wickiups and I will do my best to square this with the authorities. The time of war is over, my friend. All men must seek a better way.'

Hopkirk felt the war-chief's right hand rest on his shoulder and squeeze it; saw a look of high regard light up his deep, dark eyes. 'Always, you speak with good heart, my brother,' Diaglito said, 'and it warms me. Nevertheless, it is clear that the white man wants only war; wants only to kill all Apache. He has no respect.'

Hopkirk shook his head. 'Go to Mexico for now. There are still the old strongholds there. You will be safe while I argue with the white man on your behalf. There are men in the territory and in Washington who are willing to listen and want peace just as much as you do. It is only the men hungry for land and money who want war. Believe me, they can be stopped and controlled, but it will take time.'

Diaglito smiled, sadly. 'It is too late for us, my

friend. As you know, over the years I have done my best to help the white man and gain his trust. But how has that help and trust been repaid? He kills my son and spits on me to show his contempt. I say enough. The people of my wickiups are sheep no more.'

Hopkirk said. '*Hermano*, the white men are too many. As you now know one falls, another will quickly take his place. He is like the leaves on the trees. He will keep coming – you cannot win.'

Diaglito compressed his cruel lips. 'I know we cannot win. But if I give up now what will the white man give us? I know he will not let me live in my mountains any more, but send my warriors and me to the swamps of Florida, like he did Geronimo and his followers. My brother, I do not want to live like that.'

Hopkirk now felt Diaglito's grip tighten. 'You have tried hard to learn the ways of my people, my friend, to live as we do, to keep the peace between our two nations and I will always honour you for that. But now the time has come for you to decide your true path. You must choose whom you want to live and die with, for, from now on, you cannot live in two camps.'

Desperation filled Hopkirk. 'It does not have to be this way; things can be worked out.'

The war chief gravely shook his head. 'That day went with the death of my son and the white man's inability to give me justice.' Diaglito's black gaze softened. 'My friend, if you elect to leave us, be sure Sonseray will be safe. As her guardian and your blood brother, I will promise you that . . . always providing, of course, she does not break the customs of our people.'

Hopkirk frowned. 'But surely she will come with me, if I choose to go back to my white brethren?' he said.

'Perhaps,' Diaglito said. 'This you will have to talk over with Sonseray. Now I must leave. There is much to do.' The hand pressed down on the shoulder again. 'Think hard and choose your path well, my brother, but do not take too long over your decision. You have a week.'

Desperation flooded through Hopkirk. 'Don't do this, Diaglito.'

The war chiefs eyes held a hint of sadness. 'The decision is made, my friend. There can be no turning back.' He spun on his moccasin-clad heel and leapt on to the bare back of his piebald pony, tethered close by.

Hopkirk watched him ride away, a magnificent figure heading across the open land to the mountains. When he was but a spot in the distance Hopkirk cut down the horribly mutilated cowboy and buried him.

It was the least he could do.

CHAPTER EIGHT

As was usual on his return to the cabin he had built for Sonseray and himself in the well-watered canyon they called their home, his wife and he made love. When they were satisfied, he lay back telling her of his decision to return to his people, made on the ride here, sure she would be thrilled.

He did not receive the reaction he expected.

She sat up quickly, the look in her dark eyes one of deep hurt. 'But this cannot be, my husband. You must stay here with me. There is a child within me.'

A child?

The news rocked Hopkirk to the very roots of his being. For moments he could not find words to express his astonishment. To think he rolled out of the Navajo blankets on the pinewood bed he had made last year, placed in the corner of the warm cabin and paced over to the fire, glowing in the stone fireplace. There, standing naked facing it, he stared into the embers.

A child was what they wanted, what they craved for from the very beginning of their relationship, but right now, with the threat of war looming and the danger that came with it? The words just popped out and he immediately knew them to be stupid and arrogant.

'A child cannot be right now, Sonseray. You must be mistaken.'

Sonseray came out of the blankets, her naked, lithe form, sleek and beautiful in the fire's glow. He saw the swell on her belly and the dark bewilderment beginning to fill her dark eyes.

'You do not want the child, my husband?'

That caused impatience to rise in him. 'Yes, of course I want it. It's the timing, that's all.'

Soon as he said it he knew it was another stupid remark. He watched the hurt deepen in her eyes and the confusion. 'I do not understand, my husband. How can one time these things? Yosen wills it.'

Hopkirk found unreasonable anger filling him now, to the point of it being irrational. 'The hell he does,' he said, pacing across the earth floor like a cornered cougar. 'Dammit, Sonseray, we can't do with a child right now, you've got to be mistaken.'

He continued to pace the floor, attempting to calm himself and to think rationally.

When he had made what he considered to be a reasonable decision he said, 'Well, the child can't be born here, it's be too dangerous. It must be born at Fort Nathan. Doctor Harland Spires will attend.' He added as an attempt to reassure, 'I'm sure the birth will be all the better for that.'

Sonseray's dark face slowly lost its perplexed look and anger flashed in her dark, luminous eyes as she said, 'No, my husband! The child must be born here, in the land of the Apache. It must be Apache. There can be no other way for Sonseray.'

For the first time in their association she was challenging his judgement and he said, crisply, 'You'll obey me on this, Sonseray.'

'No, my husband, I will not!'

'I'm thinking of the child *and* you! It has to be.'

'No!'

He took a pace forward and grabbed her by the shoulders. He could not remember when Sonseray had infuriated him so much and so quickly. He felt cheated, abused in a strange way; having his authority questioned and being denied a safe environment for his child, especially now hostilities threatened. If the circumstances were different he would have been only too happy to bring up his children amongst the Apaches. He would be able to educate them, make sure they were equipped for a life beyond the wickiups, should they choose to leave when they reached maturity. He took a deep breath and gave himself time to calm himself. Then he said, 'How long to the birth?'

'Six moons.'

'Then you must come with me,' he said.

Sonseray features became stubbornly Indian and a hint of contempt came to her stare as her full lips curled up to reveal white, even teeth as well as scorn.

'Hopkirk says Sonseray must obey.' She spat on the dirt floor. 'You do not know Sonseray very well, my husband. I say the baby will be born Apache and will stay Apache.' Her stare turned even more defiant. 'You ask me to hear you; I have heard you and the answer is no. Now you must hear me. You must stay here and become full Apache if you want to play with your child before our cabin and have Sonseray as your wife.'

He shook her again. 'You will come with me, dammit,' he said, 'and I'm not asking, I'm telling.'

She tore out of his grasp and backed to the cabin wall nearest to her, eyes flashing mutiny. She drew her small skinning knife and held the blade high, posed over her heart. She said, 'Insist on this, my husband, and I will kill myself. You know Sonseray does not make idle threats.'

Hopkirk felt his stomach tighten up. Indeed, he did. He knew she would do exactly what she said she would and without hesitation if he continued to insist. He killed his anger. 'Sonseray, we must talk this through. You must realize I only want what is best for you and the child.'

He took a step forward, but Sonseray moved away and lowered the blade closer to her breast.

'What you want is not what I want, my husband,' she said. 'You do not believe I will do this?' She nicked the olive flesh of her naked breast and blood seeped and her dark eyes defied him.

'Now do you believe?'

Hopkirk held his hands up and backed off. 'I believe. All I am asking is for you to see reason.'

'Is this not what I ask of you?'

His anger exploded again. 'It's not the same, dammit!'

Fuming, he stood there and a strained silence settled in the cabin. It was broken only by the crackle and spit of the logs on the fire in the stone hearth. Flickering shadows made dancing shadows on the rough timber walls. Sonseray's image, cast on the walls, looked sinister, poised there with the knife held to her bosom.

After several seconds had passed he said, 'Does Diaglito know about the baby?'

'Yes.'

'What does he say?'

'He said only we can find the answer. I said there was only one answer to find and this was it if you fail me.' She waved the knife expressively. 'He said he hoped it would not come to that.'

'Diaglito is wise,' Hopkirk said. 'Sonseray, you have not taken enough time to think on this. Sleep on it. There are good things to be found in the white-man's world. I think you will like them when you get to know them.'

Scorn immediately registered itself on his wife's dark features as she said, 'I have experienced the white-man's world, my husband, and have found it not so good. The men look at me. Their eyes are like leeches. They violate my body with their stares. If I went to dwell amongst them ... every day I would live in fear. This is not what I want for me, or my child.'

'It is my child, too! Dammit, I will protect you!'

'I do not want to be protected against people who should be my friends.' She lifted her fine chin. 'My husband, if you think well of Sonseray and your child, then you must stay with the Apache.'

'It is not as easy as that,' he said. 'I am a white man; I must stand with white men.'

Pleading entered her eyes now. She said, 'Go up on to the mesa and think on this, my husband. It is what the men of my people do when troubled.'

He was not sure it would do any good but he dressed and stepped out of the cabin and walked up to the west rim of the plateau. There, he stared across the orange canyons stretching before him, painted in the glorious reds and purples of a sunset where the sun hung like a huge orange ball on the western horizon.

Night closed in and a coyote began to yip. Later,

he heard the cough of a panther in the canyon's darkness below. Then an owl started hooting, way to his left. Such a noise would be a very bad omen to the Apache. But to him, it was a friendly sound, soothing to the ear.

The pain of indecision within him was almost physical. He was torn right down the middle. Truth was he yearned to continue the free life he had found amongst the Apache; he achingly wanted the love of Sonseray. Yet, deep down, he realized he was still a soldier, still a white man, who, many years ago, made an oath of allegiance to serve his country, to defend it and all it stood for. Dammit, he never thought the day would come when he must chose either to dishonour that pledge or to go with it. After the capture of Geronimo he thought things were finally settled in this troubled land and the question of fidelity to one's race and beliefs would never need to be tested. God, how he had got that one wrong!

By dawn, hollow-eyed and gaunt after a night spent wrestling with his conscience, he returned to the cabin.

Sonseray was awake, sitting by the small fire. The smell of stew tugged at his hunger. She got up, filled him a bowl and handed it to him, along with a spoon and returned to her seat by the fire.

She did not look at him, did not speak to him.

After he had eaten he said, 'It is decided. I leave for Fort Nathan. I ask you to come with me, but I do not order you.'

She gave out with a little gasp, almost a whimper, and lowered her head and shook it. 'This cannot be, my husband.'

He found his hopes wither within him. In his naivety he half-expected her to cave in, change her mind. But why should she? Her loyalty to her race must be just as strong as his, maybe more so, but his disappointment was tremendous and he stood trying to come to terms with it.

Finally he said, 'I will need food for my journey to Fort Nathan.'

She still did not look at him. 'I will get it.'

Then, with an animal cry, she turned to him and went down on her knees and looked up into his face. He saw abject misery was stamped on every part of her features and it added to his already deep sorrow. She shuffled forward on her knees and grasped his hand and pressed it to her face.

'Stay, my husband, I beg you. Your child will need you. I need you.' Her face lit up. 'We can go away, into the mountains. We will be safe there.'

Now almost overwhelming wretchedness filled him. It was deep and raw and tearing at his very soul. He was hardly able to get the words out. 'It is not that I do not want to stay, Sonseray,' he said, 'I cannot.'

Sobbing deeply she crumpled at his feet. He wanted to stoop, lift her up, pull her to him and hold her and kiss her and say yes he would do as she requested, but . . . 'It will not be for ever, Sonseray,' he assured her, 'and Diaglito will look after you until I return.'

Her stare came up, fierce again.

'That is the job of my husband!'

He felt like a whipped cur as he went out of the cabin, saddled up and mounted. Soon she came to him with food and water. After she gave him the food she returned to the cabin and closed the door.

It was like she was shutting him out of her life forever, finalizing the separation, the cross-nation bonding.

He stared at the stout timbers of the door, the door he made with his own hands out of virgin pine when he built the cabin. His heart felt like a block of ice within him. He took one long last look at the home he had made for Sonseray and then wheeled his horse and went off at a canter down the canyon.

He was splashing across the stream when he became aware of movement on the west slope. He looked up to see Diaglito was guiding his piebald pony down it, through the large cluster of boulders there. On reaching bottom the war chief came towards him. Up close he said, in Apache, 'You have decided to return to your people, my brother?'

'Yes.'

71

'Sonseray is not with you?'

'No.'

'Perhaps it is for the best,' Diaglito said.

'I do not think so.' Then Hopkirk caught Diaglito's dark gaze. 'Will you talk to her, *mi hermano?*'

Diaglito shook his head. 'It is not for me to intervene.'

Hopkirk nodded and accepted Diaglito's words and clasped his brother's forearm. 'May Yosen protect you in the times ahead.'

Diaglito returned the grip with sincerity. 'And you, my brother. May our paths never cross.'

'It is so wished,' Hopkirk said.

'It is so wished,' echoed Diaglito.

It was the Apache way, Hopkirk knew, brief and to the point and totally sincere.

Two days later Hopkirk rode into Fort Nathan and offered to scout for the army. His friend Major John Dunstan greeted him with open arms, informing him that isolated Apache depredations were already taking place in the territory and his return was, to say the least, timely.

The job of chief scout was his if he wanted it.

He said that he did.

THE AFTERMATH

CHAPTER NINE

They were now into the month of June. The patrol Hopkirk was riding with was well into Apache country. As he anticipated, Diaglito moved the women and children deeper into the mountains. Even so, he found it frustrating to come upon deserted strongholds after riding for days under a burning sun and through the roughest of country, often with little food or water.

Worse still, while the women, children and the old ones trekked to these new hideouts, the best of Diaglito's braves were raiding far and wide, looting food, clothing; killing anybody who got in their way.

They moved like ghosts. After one deadly attack they would fade into the vast dry country leaving little trace of their passage only to pop up, days later and fifty miles away, to commit another raid, accompanied by the usual atrocities. It was the age-old way of the Apache, which, like so many times in the past, left the military fuming and frustrated.

Hopkirk gazed across the burning country they were travelling. These desert patrols, he knew, tested men to their limits. It was vast, empty land, but compensating for that, there were many islands of fertility. However, it was deeply frustrating to have the Apaches using mesa top lookout posts to monitor cavalry movements, then using smoke signals to warn of the direction and strength of troop dispositions.

Nevertheless, the army possessed a trick or two. Chief amongst these was the use of heliographs enabling them to make contact over long distances. Even so, when the army did have the luck to happen upon a recently used hideout it was always found deserted.

After a month of no results, Hopkirk knew the overall commander of the Department of Arizona, General Nelson Miles, was becoming increasingly irate by the lack of success. And with Fort Nathan in the middle of this cauldron of rebellion, Miles was coming down hard on John Dunstan to put all means at his disposal into hunting down Diaglito. And, in consequence, Dunstan was urging Will Hopkirk, as chief scout, to start getting some results.

However, Will did have one crumb of comfort for General Miles. Most of the warriors in other tribes were not flocking to join Diaglito, as the war chief hoped; only a few renegade Apaches were joining him. One figure bandied about claimed Diaglito could field no more than thirty braves at any one time. Even so, Hopkirk knew thirty wild Apaches on their own ground were a formidable opponent and no Indian fighter worth his salt would ever underestimate them.

Hopkirk now skimmed sweat beads off his dust-caked forehead. Long ago he came to the conclusion he would never get used to this relentless heat. He looked back at the troop, thirty strong, strung out behind him and stirring up a lot of dust. They looked like grey ghosts, the colour of their uniforms hardly discernible because of the layers of dust plastered on them.

Heading the column was the recently graduated West Pointer Lieutenant Bob James. Hopkirk was given to understand this was his first patrol and he was asked to keep an eye on the young lieutenant, which he couldn't do when he was out on a scout. So it was comforting to have the presence of his long-time friend, Sergeant Pat Ryan, along to help. Pat was an old campaigner. No doubt he would counsel the boy in the hope he would see sense.

He stared at the desert and red-rock country ahead. This section of land was truly harsh and perfect for ambush. All his instincts were telling him Diaglito was out there watching his every move.

Hopkirk slowly ranged his gaze across the heat-quivering horizon then paused; smoke was rising in an oily black column from the green, hilly country to the south. He held few doubts it was coming from the Allen ranch on Verano Creek. Even so, he wasn't too concerned about it. Like all the other settlers hereabouts, the Allen family were warned of the uprising weeks ago and advised to get themselves and their loved ones into Nathan City as soon as possible.

Surely, Jim Allen did this?

Pat Ryan, riding beside him, perked up out of his heat-induced lethargy. He said, 'What do you think?'

Hopkirk shrugged. 'Diaglito looting the place and torching it just for the hell of it?'

Ryan cracked a grin into the mask of dust on his face. 'In that case, could be we've got lucky.'

Hopkirk said, 'Inclined to agree.'

Lieutenant James, clearly hot and sweaty in his buttoned-up uniform, his blond hair dripping saline from under his campaign hat, came from the front and said, 'D'you think we should investigate?'

'Yes,' Hopkirk said. 'We could be on to him.'

An hour and a half later they topped the rise overlooking the long, low, whitewashed adobe Allen ranch house. As well as the house, all the outbuildings were smouldering, smoke-blackened ruins. However, the thing that made Hopkirk's eyelids narrow and his jaw set into a bitter line were the bodies littering the ground, and they were not the carcasses of animals.

Ryan said, his voice tight, 'I told the damned fool to go in.'

Hopkirk clamped his thin lips together, didn't reply.

They eased their tired horses down the long slope, which was matted with sun-dried grama grass. Hopkirk saw grazing beeves as specks on the brown slopes to the north. He wondered how many steers Diaglito had driven off to feed his people, though it was well known Apaches much preferred mule meat.

Arriving at the burnt-out ranch, investigation established the seven occupants – Jim and Mary Allen, their three boys, John, Frank and Nathan, their two daughters, Sybil and Josephine – had all suffered torture. Worst of all, Josephine, Sybil and Mary had clearly been raped, probably repeatedly, before meeting their death in the most horrible of ways, that of being disembowelled.

Lieutenant James promptly excused himself and threw up.

As for Hopkirk and the rest of the seasoned patrol . . . the dead were dead; that could not be changed and life went on. More practically Hopkirk knew the patrol needed water and it was policy to top up canteens whenever it became available. He went to the well. He was not surprised to see the water contaminated with the carcasses of the Allen ranch's pigs.

Ryan peered into the well with him and said, 'True to form.' Then he gazed around the hills with serious grey eyes and added, 'He's close, Will. I feel it.'

Hopkirk nodded, soberly. 'So do I.'

Seeing Lieutenant James was still indisposed Ryan ordered graves to be dug. After he got the men to work, Hopkirk said to him, 'Watch out for James, Pat. I'm going out.'

He now approached the recovering James and informed him of his intentions. James nodded his agreement and said, 'For God's sake find this heathen, Will!'

Hopkirk said, 'I'll do my damnedest; you can bet on that.'

He rode out and circled the ranch, hunting for sign. He knew Diaglito was never going to make finding him easy; however, after some persistence he found indications suggesting Diaglito's party were heading for canyon country. But coming upon such obvious tracks caused suspicion to rise in Hopkirk. Apaches seldom left such a clear trail to follow. But there was one possibility: Diaglito was feeling confident and didn't think he needed to be careful? However, there was also another much more sinister reason: Diaglito *wanted* his tracks to be found.

Hopkirk narrowed his eyelids and searched the horizons around him with vigilant eyes. And that was a different ball game altogether.

*

When he returned to the ranch Lieutenant James was saying prayers over the freshly filled-in graves. Hopkirk dismounted and removed his hat, bowed his head and placed his clasped hands in his lap. When James was through he looked up. It seemed to Hopkirk James had aged ten years this last hour.

'Well?' the lieutenant said.

'There's tracks out yonder; I need to follow them up.'

'Diaglito's?'

'Can't be certain, but it's Apaches, that's for sure.'

James said, 'I think it would be a mistake for you to follow them alone.'

Hopkirk shook his head. 'One man makes less dust. What I suggest is, you wait here for an hour and then follow me. When I have something, I'll find you.'

'I still think it is folly,' James said. 'We should go together.'

Hopkirk said, 'You'll have to trust me on this.'

He turned and looked for Pat Ryan. He saw the chunky sergeant was checking the harness on his big grey stallion.

He mounted and rode over. 'I'm going out again, Pat. I think it's more than likely Diaglito is up ahead.' He flicked a glance in the young lieutenant's direction. 'Don't allow him to do anything foolish while I'm gone, uh?'

Ryan compressed his dust-caked lips. 'I'll do my best, bucko, but at the end of the day 'tis he who gives the orders.'

Hopkirk nodded. 'Do your best.'

'Don't worry about that,' Ryan said. ''Tis my neck on the block, too.'

Hopkirk kicked flanks and cantered toward the place he picked up sign earlier. He was tingling with anticipation. It was their first break against his shrewd and cunning blood brother.

He wasn't going to waste it.

CHAPTER TEN

Past noon the following day and Pat Ryan was feeling anxious. Will Hopkirk's tracks had petered out last evening leaving himself and Lieutenant James uncertain as to what to do. Ryan suspected the tracks were brushed out and that only posed another mystery ... by whom? Nevertheless, he advised Lieutenant James to carry on in their general direction until night camp was made. When it was, extra sentries were posted and no fires were lit.

The night passed in edgy silence, men chewing on hardtack washed down with alkali-bitter water before fading into fitful sleep. They broke camp an hour before sun up, still riding in the general direction Hopkirk's tracks were going before they found them wiped out.

By this time the patrol was now almost into canyon country and Ryan looked about him nervously. Dammit, Will Hopkirk should have been back hours ago.

He cursed the dust rising around him, lifted by the hoofs of the patrol's tired horses. It got into a man's nostrils, filtered into his mouth and throat; found its way into every nook and cranny of his body, and all aggravated by the sun, which was a pale, baleful orb above them, suspended in a washed-out sky. He set his chin into a stern line. He would never get used to this damned heat.

He looked about him. Since Hopkirk's tracks had disappeared some sixth sense kept telling him all was not well. It was nothing tangible, just a prickling feeling up his backbone, a tingling in his gut, though neither of which made any rational sense. It was just some primeval instinct.

Once more he allowed his red-rimmed, dust-sore eyes to search the area, but it was the ever-watchful Trooper Boskat Neil riding by his side who spotted them first. 'Apache, in the mouth of the canyon to our left, Sergeant . . . whole bunch of them.'

Ryan flicked his gaze in the direction of Neil's nod. He saw six braves strung out across the narrow mouth of the canyon, maybe a hundred yards away. They were like ghosts, Ryan fumed silently – just came out of nothing. Worse, this bunch was painted for war.

Ryan kept his stare on the group. As soon as they realized they'd got the soldiers' attention the braves began jeering and making obscene gestures while circling their ponies and waving their war lances, rifles and warbows.

Lieutenant James, heading the column, turned. Ryan noticed his startling blue eyes were lit up with excitement. He seemed hardly able to contain it. 'By God, at last,' he said, as he came close, 'a sight of the red heathen. I do believe we have them, Sergeant Ryan. Get the men ready to attack.'

A cold hand clamped Ryan's stomach. He raised a gnarled hand and smiled a patient smile. 'Easy now, sir, not so fast, this could be a trap.'

James stared, as if dumbfounded. 'Are you disobeying a direct order, Sergeant Ryan?'

'No, sir, not at all,' Ryan said. 'It's just that the Apache is cunning and I think this is not what it seems.'

James frowned. 'I don't follow you.'

Ryan pointed out the tall, deep-chested brave with the hooked nose and the jet-black eyes in front of the group. 'That's Diaglito. I think he wants us to follow him into that canyon. It's an old Indian trick, so don't fall for it. Find open ground and make him fight on your terms, not his.'

James said, 'Diaglito? By God.'

His lips thinned and set into hard lines. The hatred Ryan saw in the lieutenant's eyes when he viewed the massacre at the Allen ranch yesterday afternoon manifested itself once more in them. The boy stared raptly at the war chief. Ryan knew this was his first sighting of the famed White Mountain Apache.

After moments James said, 'Why, he's nothing but a savage.'

Ryan said, 'Don't be fooled by appearances, sir. Diaglito is clever. Above all, don't go after him into that canyon.'

James's stare was puzzled when Ryan met it. 'Why? Dammit, Sergeant, we've run the murderous heathen to earth! We must attack him! What we found on Verano Creek yesterday demands nothing less. What the devil's got into you, man? Have you lost your nerve?'

Ryan held back his anger with difficulty. Few men suggested Pat Ryan was a coward with impunity. However, an officer was an officer and this was Pat Ryan's last patrol. After this one he was mustering out with twenty-six years' continuous service under his belt. He needed to go out with his stripes intact, his record unblemished and his meagre pension intact.

'No, sir,' he said. 'I say what I say only because I have seen this kind of thing before. That red devil will skin you alive if you go after him. He'll have his whole band in that canyon, waiting for you.'

James's young face curled into a faint sneer. 'Such subtlety from a savage I find hard to believe, Sergeant.' He chin lifted slightly, a little superciliously. 'So, what do you suggest? We sit here and do nothing? That is not an option, I assure you.'

'No, sir,' Ryan said. 'All I'm saying is, we make him fight on our terms.'

He pointed to a cluster of orange boulders half a mile distant, across the intermediate land shimmering in the heat. 'Take up a defensive position amongst those rocks and stand him off until Will Hopkirk rejoins the patrol. He'll have some ideas as to how best to deal with Diaglito.'

James's stare was indignant. 'Meaning I haven't, Sergeant?'

'Not at all, sir,' Ryan said. 'It is just that Will Hopkirk lived with those people for five years. He knows them better than any man I know. And if I may remind you, before we left Fort Nathan, Major Dunstan suggested you listen to Hopkirk's advice before taking any action against Diaglito, due to your lack of experience in dealing with them in the field.'

Ryan cast a nervous glance at the Apaches. They were clearly getting more agitated at the patrol's lack of response. But James did not seem to notice. He said, almost petulantly, 'There is no need to remind me, Sergeant. I recall the directive perfectly well.' He began fidgeting with the reins on his horse. After moments he lifted his chin and said, 'Do you want to know what I think, Sergeant? I think Hopkirk has gone completely wild and has gone back to his friend Diaglito . . . if he ever left him. I think Hopkirk has delivered us straight into his hands.'

Ryan stared with eyes that looked like chips of flint. 'That's ridiculous, sir. Will Hopkirk is a man of the highest integrity. He would never dream of doing such a thing.'

James's smile was faintly patronizing. 'Wouldn't he?' he said. 'Well, I'm inclined to think otherwise, Sergeant. Tell me, why do you think he is missing if you have such faith in him?'

Though resenting the lieutenant's tone Ryan said, 'My fancy is he went out to count Diaglito's numbers so he could figure out the best way to deal with him. That takes a deal of nerve and time and that is why we should head for the rocks and wait for him to return. As for Diaglito knowing where we are? My guess is that wily spalpeen has known our position from the moment we rode out of Fort Nathan three days ago. He won't need Will Hopkirk to tell him that.'

James frowned. 'I find that hard to believe, Sergeant.' He waved a hand toward the now milling and clearly angry Apaches. 'I think you are giving those red heathens far too much respect. I think Diaglito has run into us by mistake and by using bravado is making the best of it.'

Ryan decided it was time to acquaint rookie James with a few facts about those *red heathens*. 'Sir, the Apache seldom does anything by mistake. He is a devious and resourceful enemy and his stamina is legendary. If pursued he will ride his horse to death, and then slit its throat and drink its blood. After that he will cut off choice portions of the beast and set to running once more, eating the raw meat on the way. They say he can out-run a horse over distance. Indeed, they have been known to sprint fifty miles in a day on foot with little water and in the hottest of desert country. And, as well as being a chronic thief, the Apache is the classic guerrilla fighter. He rarely fights on open ground because he lacks numbers. He prefers stealth, ambush, and he is a master at concealing himself. He will rise up from a seemingly empty desert and have you sliced, crotch to breastbone, before you have time to blink. Make no bones about it, he is a deadly opponent. Do not underestimate him and, above all, do not fall for his murderous games.'

James again stared at the Apaches, but this time Ryan saw there was a thoughtful look on his face. After moments the lieutenant sighed and raised his sandy brows and said, 'Very well, Sergeant, I will bow to your experience. We will head for those rocks as you advise and take up defensive—'

A whirring noise whipped past Ryan's ear and James flinched and swayed aside, as if the object had hissed past him too, cutting off what else he was about to say. And within the compass of that same instant the flat crack of a rifle sounded, sending echoes bouncing into the desolate canyon country beyond. Further, Trooper Ben Lawson, a dozen yards back and to the left of Lieutenant James, gave out with a harsh yell and clutched his chest and toppled out of his saddle.

Adding to this sudden mayhem the lieutenant's roan mare began rearing and kicking causing James to wrestle with the beast while having the presence of mind to shout, 'Return fire, men . . . Soames, see what you can do for Lawson.'

'Yes, sir!' Soames said.

He swung out of the saddle and went down on one knee beside the fallen trooper. He quickly felt for the pulse in his neck. After moments he looked up. 'Looks to me Lawson's dead, sir.'

James, still trying to control his startled horse, said, 'Very well, Trooper, remount and commence firing.'

'Yes, sir!'

While this was going on, Ryan watched the whooping Apaches wheel their ponies and begin riding for the canyon. But despite the two volleys that followed them Ryan was disappointed to see not one of the devils drop out of his blanket saddle. However, one did sway, obviously hit.

Cursing under his breath, Ryan sighted up on to the last of the retreating bucks dusting into the canyon's black maw. He pressed the trigger. His army issue Spencer carbine boomed and bucked against his shoulder. Satisfaction filled him as he saw the .50 calibre bullet punch the Apache out of his blanket saddle and into the boiling dust. The buck did not move again.

The firing from the rest of the patrol petered out as the last of the braves disappeared into the canyon.

Ryan wiped bitter dust off his dry mouth with a slightly shaking hand and looked for Lieutenant James. The young man was now in charge of his mount and appeared to be in full control of his nerves. That pleased Ryan. The boy was showing some mettle. One day, with a little guidance, he might make a fine officer.

James rode up to him, his startlingly blue eyes excited again. 'I have a strong feeling that bullet was meant for me, Sergeant.'

Ryan said, 'I think maybe you're right.' He attempted to smile while he mopped his brows and neck with his neckerchief. 'Get rid of the chiefs first, uh, sir?' But judging by the look that came to James's youthful face he clearly did not appreciate his dry humour.

James said, 'Crudely put, Sergeant, but yes.' He raised fine, sandy brows. 'But with regard to not going after them . . . by God, this changes my mind. I will have no more shilly-shallying, Sergeant, no more indecision, no more showing of respect for those murdering heathens and no more waiting for a scout to make the decision. We go into that canyon, now.'

Ryan grabbed hold of the lieutenant's arm. 'Ah, for the love of God, sir, don't do it; it will be murder. Head for the rocks. We'll stand off the red devils, never fear.'

James angrily snatched his arm away. 'Let me remind you, Sergeant Ryan, that we are fighting men. We will have our revenge for the death of Lawson and the deaths of the Allen family on Verano Creek.' He lifted his chin. 'Now, sir, you will do your duty, or you will know the consequences when we return to Fort Nathan. Do I make myself clear?'

Twenty-six years of near blind obedience to orders kicked in and Sergeant Pat Ryan saluted.

'Clear as day, sir!'

James nodded. 'Good. Now give the order, Sergeant.'

'Yes, sir!'

But in that moment Ryan felt his whole world collapsing about him. His dreams of what he was going to do after mustering out at the end of this patrol; the wounds he received in the defence of his country; the pension – such as was – he was to collect after twenty-six years of hard soldiering; Ryan's Drop Inn . . . the place he planned to open using his savings in some quiet garrison town when he mustered out. Were his ambitions to end here in this grubby little canyon in Arizona? It appeared it was going to be a soldier's end for Pat Ryan after all.

He turned stiffly in the saddle and stared at the waiting column behind. He waved his long-barrelled Cavalry Colt above his head and yelled, 'Right, boys, let's be after them, and may God be with you!'

CHAPTER ELEVEN

According to the reading on Ryan's half-hunter watch his father had handed to him before he sailed from Liverpool, England, to the New World twenty-eight years ago, it was close on midnight. Near to exhaustion, Ryan stared at the near full moon and the vast array of twinkling stars that formed a canopy above the horizons of the canyon. Then he pulled a big grubby right hand through his dark, grey-streaked locks. Jesus, but he was tired.

He wrinkled his nose at the pungent smell of burnt gunpowder, the stench of blood and stale excreta that still lingered. Then he stared at the bodies of the dead troopers littering the floor of the canyon. His heart bled for those brave boys. He should have been one of them and only God knew why he wasn't.

The red bastards were on the plateau above now. He could hear the beating of their drums, the chanting of the braves. It was a din of savage celebration. And mingled amongst the noise was the warbling of the women.

Some were no doubt mourning the deaths of their menfolk. Their quavering falsettos brought grim satisfaction to Ryan. His boys had given those red heathen one hell of a fight this afternoon, no doubt about that. His heart swelled with pride. Each man had sold his life dearly. He was damned proud of them.

Now he attempted to shrug off this relentless gnawing fatigue that was eating into him and stared at the three wounded troopers nearby amongst the rocks. One of them was whimpering quietly.

The sound filled Ryan with a feeling of helplessness. He could do little to help the man. There was no laudanum, no dressings, nothing. The supply wagon holding food, water, and medical supplies had gone up in flames minutes after the first deadly Apache attack, when lead and fire arrows rained down on them from the rocky slopes of the canyon. Half the column fell in that first clash, either badly wounded or dead. Lieutenant James did his best to organize resistance, but in reality, it was chaos for the first couple of minutes.

In the second rush, the Apaches killed the horse holders and took the horses. Instantly, lithe Apache boys came out of the rocks waving sticks and shouting as they hurried the animals away down the canyon, leaving the braves to return to try and finish off the column.

But after the initial shock of the onslaught the men found cover fast. Nevertheless, the murderous fire of the Apaches continued to pour down on them, slowly picking them off one by one throughout the furnace-hot afternoon. When sunset slashed stark lines of orange and red across the sky and dark began to settle, the firing petered out. The silence that followed was worse than the sounds of battle. Men still strained to catch a glimpse of bronzed muscular bodies filtering down through the boulders. It was only when they heard the chants of victory starting up on the plateau that they realized fighting was maybe over for the day.

Now Ryan felt a great emptiness within him as he stared at the dead. Don't any man ever again tell Pat Ryan the Apache can't shoot straight, or can't organize himself when involved in an affray such as this.

But out of his emptiness came anger. He clenched his hands into big, gnarled fists. Dammit, where the hell was Will Hopkirk? It wasn't like that tall, lean scout to let the column down like this.

Startling Ryan, a coyote yipped . . . way up the canyon. It was answered with a long, mournful howl.

Coming to acute alertness Ryan narrowed eyelids and licked dry lips. He wondered if they were really those opportunist scavengers, come to feed off the dead? Or were they Apaches communicating while moving in to finish off what was left of the column?

Ryan found himself doubting the latter. He knew enough about Apaches to know they did not like fighting at night. And people professing to know them said it was something to do with not being able to find their way to their Apache heaven in the dark, should they be killed. But Ryan also knew it was not unknown for Apaches to sneak in under cover of darkness, when there was little risk to themselves, and cut a throat or two and sneak out again just for the hell of it.

He stared at Lieutenant James's body, lying silent in death close by. The Apache war lance that had killed him was still embedded in his chest. It stood stark as an exclamation mark against the bright, moonlit sky. The impalement happened during the second charge. A fierce death-thrust, made from the back of a charging pony by a shrieking buck, drove the spear right through the boy's heart, skewering him to the sandy soil. At least the death was quick and—

Loose pebbles rattled above Ryan. A sensation like icy water began trickling down his backbone. He pushed himself upright, off the big boulder he was leaning against. His ears twitched as he tried to pick up more sound. It could be natural erosion, but it could be something much more sinister.

Sweating profusely and hardly daring to breathe,

he reached for his Spencer carbine. He knew it was fully loaded. After four years fighting the forces of the Confederacy, ten years battling with the Sioux and Northern Cheyenne in the Dakota and Montana territories, and now eight years chasing the deadly Apache, he was never without a loaded gun near to hand.

He peered into the night, widening his gaze to try and get more clarity to his vision, but he could see nothing; hear nothing. But this sixth sense of his was warning him things were not right out there. He could feel it. Something real and dangerous was lurking in those dark shadows.

When the attack came it was abrupt and savage. Fingers reaching over his face from behind and sinking into the grizzled flesh under his cleft chin and hauling his head back to expose his thick throat. He didn't even have the time to cry out, the assault was so sudden.

He dropped his rifle. It clattered on to the pebbly soil. He reached up with his big hands to grasp the arm, which was holding a big Bowie knife and was descending towards his exposed neck with gut-wrenching swiftness.

He wrestled with the arm, trying to steer the blade away from its clear intention – to slash open Pat Ryan's throat from ear to ear. The power in it was the equal of his, if not a shade stronger. But it was with odd clarity he saw the blade now straining near his Adam's apple bore the hallmark of Sheffield steel. There was only one knife like that as he knew of around these parts. . . .

'Hopkirk, it's me, Ryan!'

For a moment the steel-like fingers remained fastened on his flesh, then they relaxed and fell away, as did the blade. Ryan sensed the presence behind him moving back, breathing hard.

Hopkirk croaked, 'Pat? I thought you were all to be dead down here. I figured you were some thieving buck who'd dressed himself up in soldier-boy kit and was intent on robbing the rest of the bodies.'

Ryan flopped forward, gagging for air. When he finally got his breath back he said, 'Do I look like a damn Apache?'

He turned to glare at Hopkirk and gasped at what he saw. Hopkirk's naked body, pale and ghostly in the strong moonlight, was crisscrossed with shallow, but obvious knife slashes. Not deep, but some were still seeping blood. However, that wasn't all. The scout's hawkish features were a mass of swollen flesh and vivid weals daubed purple lines across his bruised flesh. It was plain to see those weals were made by whips wielded with some force.

'God, Will,' he said, 'what happened to you?'

Hopkirk's reply still came as a brittle croaking. 'The Three Deaths the Apache call it. It's reserved for warriors whom they think will die well. First they soften you up with their quirts and blows from wooden staves, then they singe you with firebrands. After that comes the cutting and stabbing with knives and lances . . . but not too deep; you might bleed to death and that would spoil the last and greatest entertainment: trial by fire. Staking a man out and placing burning ashes on the most vulnerable parts of his body and left there – to be renewed when required – while it eats into his flesh. At this juncture the braves usually sit around observing and discussing their victim's lack of fortitude, or otherwise. To die well is always applauded, but to die screaming like a woman is treated with the utmost contempt.'

'And you lived with those sons of bitches?'

'Diaglito is not a son of a bitch, Pat.'

'He is to me, dammit.'

'This is old ground, Pat, and this isn't the time to bring it up.'

Ryan grunted and fumbled for his canteen and passed over. 'Have a drink of water, you look as though you need it.'

Hopkirk took the canteen and drank deeply.

While he was doing so Ryan said, 'Just to satisfy my own curiosity; how did they manage to catch you?'

Hopkirk finished drinking and carefully wiped his bruised and split mouth with the back of a grubby hand. 'Yesterday, four miles beyond the Allen place; Diaglito and his bucks were waiting for me.' He shook his head ruefully despite the state it was in. 'Dammit, Pat, I thought I was better than that.'

Ryan said, 'Seems you weren't. How did you escape? It don't usually happen with Apaches, once they get their hands on you.'

'Sonseray, my wife, freed me.'

Ryan opened his wrinkled eyelids and gave Hopkirk a stare of disbelief. 'You mean to say you married one of those red sons of b. . . ?' Ryan bit off the rest of the crude expletive and added, 'Well, you sure kept that one quiet. And here was me thinking you were my friend.'

'She's a fine lady, Pat, and I love her deeply. I think you'd like her when you get to know her.'

Ryan sighed. 'Aye, well, I guess a man makes his own choosing at the end of the day. Who is Patrick Ryan to judge? And right at this moment we've got a lot more urgent things to worry about.'

Ryan studied the sweat and streaks of blood glistening on Hopkirk's body. He came to the opinion the pain Hopkirk was suffering right now must be acute, but there was little sign that the big ex-army captain and now chief scout for Fort Nathan was ever going to show that.

He said, 'What do you reckon to our chances?'

Hopkirk gave him a long, hard look then took another swig from the canteen before he said, 'How many men survived, Pat?'

Ryan pursed thick lips. 'Nine fit to travel, including me. Three men are wounded, but I doubt they'll make it through the night. The rest are dead.'

Hopkirk said, 'Lieutenant James?'

'Lance through the heart on the second charge.' Ryan pointed a stubby finger. 'Over there.'

Hopkirk turned. For a moment Ryan thought he saw genuine regret register itself on Hopkirk's brutally battered features when he saw the lieutenant's carcass lying in the moonlight.

After moments the scout said, 'Dammit, I promised John Dunstan I would look out for him.' His gaze lifted and Ryan met it. 'I hope you tried to talk him out of it, Pat?'

'Sure I did, but, in the end, he wouldn't take the advice I gave him.'

Hopkirk sighed again. 'Well, he isn't the first rookie lieutenant to do that,' he said. He looked about him. After moments he said, 'Where's the supply wagon? I could do with disinfecting and dressing these wounds.'

Ryan waved at the pile of still glowing ashes fifty yards away. 'There, bucko, what's left of it.'

He saw bitter disappointment come to Hopkirk's battered features, but after moments the scout looked up hopefully. 'Where's your flask, Pat? The one that isn't regulation.'

Though Ryan grinned at Hopkirk's perception,

the punishment could be severe if a man was found carrying strong liquor on patrol. 'You do appreciate 'tis only for medicinal purposes, bucko,' he said.

Hopkirk attempted a return smile but grimaced instead. 'Didn't think it was for anything else.'

'Good enough.' Ryan pulled out the flask from the big pocket inside his dusty, sweaty and torn tunic. 'Want me to clean up those cuts for you, bucko?'

Hopkirk's look was grateful. 'Guess it would make things easier.'

Ryan got to work. Hopkirk groaned and gasped as Pat wiped away the blood and grime from the wounds and dug out the grit and soil, while disinfecting the wounds with the high proof alcohol. When the cleaning was over Ryan looked keenly into the scout's grey eyes and offered the flask. 'I guess you'll be needing a belt of this now, uh, bucko?'

'I could use a little right now.'

Holding the flask in a shaking hand Hopkirk raised it to his swollen lips and drank gratefully. Returning the vessel he said, 'How many able-bodied men have we got, Pat?'

'Troopers Bosket Neil, Martin Lish, Wyatt Lickmore, Curtis French, Harvey Kitts, Roger Coots, John Puckas and Peter Simms.'

'The wounded?' Hopkirk said.

'Johnson, Purcell and Rodham.'

'Their chances?'

'Not good.'

'Check them,' said Hopkirk, 'and hope they're dead.'

Ryan frowned. 'That's an odd thing to say, bucko.'

'We can't carry wounded, Pat.'

Ryan stared into Hopkirk's battered yet determined face. 'You mean you're thinking of getting out of here?'

'Any reason why we shouldn't?'

Ryan allowed his incredulity full flow as he said, 'Dammit, Will, we're surrounded, afoot! We wouldn't stand a chance if we tried to break out. Those Apache have got to be covering every exit out of here.' He shook his head. 'No, it would be better to fort up and battle it out and wait for a relief column to arrive. Major Dunstan must be thinking about sending one out by now; we're long overdue.'

Hopkirk shook his head. 'Can't risk it. They'll cut us down piecemeal from above if we hole up down here. I've got a better plan. We'll get to our horses and ride out of here.'

Ryan squinted. 'Are you serious?'

'Never more so,' Hopkirk said. 'I know where those horses are; I know where the lookouts are. Think about it, Pat . . . it'll be the last thing they'll be expecting us to do.'

Ryan narrowed his eyelids. Indeed, the plan was

sound, but there was still one other matter. 'I'll ask you again, Will . . . what about the wounded?'

'They have to stay.'

Ryan's grizzled features set into grim lines. 'Damn it, I've trained those boys. They trust me. I can't leave them.'

'We must,' Hopkirk said.

Irish stubbornness rose in Pat. 'Something you're forgetting, bucko; I'm in command here now Lieutenant James is dead and this is my decision: we carry the boys out, one way or the other.'

Hopkirk said, 'Figure we'd come round to this, Pat, eventually. The fact is General Nelson Miles restored my commission a month ago at the request of Major Dunstan, but I chose to keep it quiet.' He heaved a sigh. 'Pat, the responsibility for the fate of this patrol is now in my hands. I'm not prepared to trade nine men's lives for the sake of three, who, on your own admission, are going to die anyway.' He met Ryan's hard stare. 'Now, inform the men and get ready to move out in fifteen minutes. Ask them to gather as much food and water and ammo as they can carry. After that tell the wounded of my decision. Explain to them each man keeps his rifle and pistol, if he has one, and ten rounds of ammunition to use as he sees fit.'

'Suicide, is it, bucko?'

Hopkirk could barely meet Ryan's stare. 'Whichever way the men choose to go. But tell them enough water and food will be left to last them three days. A column should reach them by then.'

Ryan compressed his lips. 'Guess this kind of decision is what makes an officer, huh, bucko?' he said, bitterly, and moved off into the night.

Hopkirk stared after him. 'Don't think it's easy, Pat,' he said quietly.

CHAPTER TWELVE

Now Hopkirk looked down at the wounds criss-crossing his torso. Flies were buzzing all over them, feasting on the blood-seeping flesh. That wasn't good. He needed to get those wounds covered.

He moved amongst the dead, looking for clean linen. He found a shirt and pants and pulled them on trying to ignore the pain it caused. Now he pushed his English steel Bowie knife – Sonseray had given it to him after she had freed him – into the belt he found to hold up his britches. After that he stooped and picked up a standard issue trapdoor Springfield rifle. It was lying in the dust close by an arrow-pierced trooper whose dead eyes stared up at him accusingly as he took the weapon. Then he found cartridges for the weapon and pocketed them. After that he prised Lieutenant James's engraved single-action Smith & Wesson Schofield six-shooter out of his slim white hand and loaded the handsome piece, using shells he found in

James's ammunition pouch. The surplus bullets he placed in a separate pocket.

Feeling safer now he was fully armed, he looked over the moonlit sandy floor of the canyon. Corpses sprawled in grotesque positions everywhere. The smell of blood and shattered flesh pervaded the area. He knew the stench would get worse, much worse.

Dammit, he should have stayed with the patrol. He would have used his rank to stop James entering this canyon. He now realized it was a silly move asking Pat to talk the lieutenant out of any foolish action until he got back. End of the day, after twenty-six years' service and with perhaps painful reminders that discipline was everything in this man's modern army, Pat Ryan was conditioned to obey orders.

Just then, Pat came out of the night. 'The wounded,' he said, 'I've checked on them. They're all dead.'

'I've got to say I find that a relief. So . . . are the men ready to move?'

'They are.'

'Gather them around, Pat.'

When the troopers were assembled Hopkirk ran his gaze over them – dusty, blood-smeared and tired men. He gazed into their grim faces, their staring eyes. He saw most of those looks still held the hell of the afternoon in them.

He said, 'Has Sergeant Ryan informed you of my taking command?'

Bosket Neil, the tall, painfully thin former Missouri backwoodsman with the large, bobbing Adam's apple, said 'Yes . . . sir.'

The rest of the group just shuffled and cast indifferent stares in his direction. Hopkirk guessed by their looks and actions what they were thinking . . . it really didn't matter a damn who it was that was going to lead them, right now they were in a fix they likely wouldn't get out of. Hopkirk decided they needed cheering up.

He said, 'Men, we're going to get out of this alive.'

His words were met with silence, just stony, disbelieving looks.

'You hear me?' he said.

Trooper Martin Lish, a one-time failed Kansas farmer, said, 'Easy saying, sir, but we ain't got horses, and not a lot of water. And we got wounded.'

Hopkirk said, 'The wounded are dead and we'll get horses and water.'

Trooper Wyatt Lickmore, a tall, forty-four-year-old loose-limbed Texan said, 'Just how d'you propose to do it, sir?'

Hopkirk's normally aquiline, but now grossly bruised features, set into what could be passed as steely determination. And the grey eyes behind the swellings were ice-hard as he swept his gaze across the troopers' grim faces. 'This way: come dawn Diaglito will be riding into this canyon with the intention of finishing us off. Well, we won't be here to greet him, we'll be up on the plateau taking back our horses.'

A gasp broke from the gathering and hopeful glances were exchanged before they diverted back to Hopkirk.

Will gazed around the group. 'Now, men, let me acquaint you with the rest of the plan. When we've got the horses, I calculate we'll have about an hour to put some distance between Diaglito and us. However, once Diaglito realizes he's been fooled he's going to come after us as though all the devils in hell are at his ass. But, rest assured, we're going to make it as difficult as possible for him all the way to Fort Nathan.'

Trooper Wyatt Lickmore said, 'Well, God's truth, it's a hell of a scheme.'

Hopkirk nodded. 'And what's more, Lickmore, it'll work.'

Trooper Martin Lish looked at the corpses littering the canyon floor. 'What about the dead . . . do we bury 'em?'

Hopkirk shook his head. 'We haven't the time. We will have to leave them to God's good grace until a burial detail can be sent out from Fort Nathan.'

Wyatt Lickmore spat tobacco juice and nodded. 'Can't be any other way, I guess, though it sticks in the craw.'

110

Hopkirk stared around him through the silver moonlight. 'Right, men,' he said, 'let's get out of here.'

'Amen to that,' Trooper Lickmore said.

CHAPTER THIRTEEN

Dawn on this June day in the high country came in cold and fine. The remaining men of the patrol were now lying belly-flat and shivering on top of the juniper-covered red bluff rearing up at the north end of this plateau upon which Diaglito and his followers built their small, temporary wickiups and made their celebrations.

Hopkirk stared at the scene below, in the bowl of the plateau. Squaws were moving about down there, mostly poking low overnight fires into life and stirring cook pots. Some vessels were simmering on fires already ablaze.

Dogs were running around yapping. Squealing children played. Woodsmoke rose in straight lines into the cobalt-blue sky. The sun was a huge ball sitting on the horizon to the east, colouring what clouds there were to warm pale gold.

A few bucks were coming out of wickiups rubbing eyes, stretching limbs and shaking heads, heads no doubt still throbbing from the overindulgence in tizwin or tulapai, the potent native brews.

Hopkirk looked for Sonseray, but could not see her. He wasn't surprised. She must surely have quit camp and gone into hiding after releasing him. He knew that she had risked all to free him. Adopted daughter or not, Diaglito would order her death. More than likely he would do the deed himself, to give her a quick end. Others would not be so kind if it was left to them.

Waiting on this bluff Hopkirk allowed his thoughts to go back to those tense moments when Sonseray had cut the rawhide bonds holding him to the torture pole.

Soon as he was free he had staggered down from the mound the stake was on and fell into the grass, shivering with the trauma of the raw pain he was suffering. Several minutes he lay there gathering his strength, trying to deny the existence of his many hurts so that he could function properly. When he felt able he got up and looked back at the stake he was tied to. It was placed a good 200 yards from the camp. There were wild celebrations going on over there and there was no indication their movements attracted attention.

For moments he gazed at the wooden pole. It seemed to stand like a sentinel on that bare moon-lit hillock.

Sonseray had said, her eyes round, excited,

liquid-dark orbs, 'I have horses waiting in the trees, my husband. We will go into the mountains far to the north where we will not be found. Then, some day, when this is over, we will return and live in peace in our canyon.'

Her dark eyes gleamed with love.

He was still in some shock. Minutes ago, he didn't for one moment ever believe he would be getting out of this alive. However, if by some miracle he did, he had plans. But how could he tell Sonseray of them? Just now she had risked everything to give him freedom. Nevertheless, weeks ago he undertook to serve the army and consequently the boys of the patrol, painful though it was to announce that now to his wife.

As tenderly as he could, he took her serene face into his bloodied hands. 'Sonseray, what you say is a thing I want above all others, but it cannot be, not yet.'

His voice rasped on the dryness in his throat, the result of a burning hot day tied to the stake without water. 'I must go down into the canyon, to where the big fight was this afternoon.'

With a swift movement, she moved away from him. Her dark eyes were filled with disbelief. After moments she said, 'If you do, Diaglito will kill you and this will be for nothing.'

At that moment Hopkirk began to know the meaning of deep misery. He searched desperately for words to pacify her. 'I have to know if there are any men left alive down there. It is my duty to do so. If there is, they will need me.'

Her black stare flashed anger. '*I* need you, my husband! Your child needs you! Have you forgotten so soon?'

'Of course not,' he said. 'Don't make it difficult for me, Sonseray.'

'Difficult? I am your wife!' She spat on the ground. 'Who cares what happens to the white pony soldiers who murder my people?'

'I do, Sonseray. I have to.'

Her open palm struck him, hard and solid, across his swollen and cut face. The power of the blow sent new pain searing through him. But he did not react, except to reach up and feel the spot. Indeed, he felt he deserved the blow. He stepped forward. He tried to take her in his arms but she stepped back, her eyes glittering fiercely in the light from the distant camp-fires.

'No!' she said. 'Keep away. I do not want you!'

He lowered his arms to his sides. His body was quivering and it was not only because of the trauma of intense pain. Though feeling deeply wretched he said, 'I have to do this, Sonseray. It can be no other way.'

Her cry was one of pure animal anguish as she turned from him and ran into the night. He thought he could hear her sobbing. The sound of her unhappiness cut him to the quick.

A minute later came the soft thud of hoofs beating a rhythm into the darkness. Then the night became empty and soulless.

Bringing him back to the present, the crack of a rifle caused his attention to once more focus on the camp below. The source of the noise was a buck; riding around, clearly drunk and whooping like a banshee and firing his rifle into the air.

Diaglito came out of his wickiup and stared at the sunrise, tall and proud and fierce in new day's light. Talks With Birds, his wife, came forward, gave him a bowl of food. Hopkirk watched his blood brother stand and eat the meal while he stared at the pole to which he was tied yesterday. Hopkirk knew the most exquisite of all the tortures – death by fire – should have happened today, after what remained of the patrol were slaughtered in the canyon. Dammit, he wasn't sorry to deprive his blood brother of that pleasure!

Boys came riding into camp, chivvying a remuda of wiry Indian ponies before them, clearly brought in from their overnight grazing grounds.

Having camped here on several occasions in the past in happier times, Hopkirk knew there was a couple of *tinajas* – seepages of water – about three-quarters of a mile to the east of the camp. The grass and trees was green and succulent up there.

Thinking of horses ... Hopkirk stared across the plateau at the grove of cottonwoods around the other *tinaja* on this plain, a mile to the north.

The patrol's horses, he knew, were held there. Hanging on the torture pole yesterday, through battered eyes he watched the horses driven there by the boys who must have taken them off the braves who had cut them out while the battle raged down there in the canyon.

Using Ryan's field-glass he patiently surveyed the cropping beasts. He counted four boys watching them. But at the moment they were playing a wrestling game. The horses were taking second place in their attentions.

But then shrill, wild whoops turned his attention back to the village. He saw there was increasing activity down there. About twenty bucks were now amongst the remuda the boys had brought in and were catching their ponies. Mounted, they began riding around the village yelling and waving their rifles, bows, six-guns and war lances.

Squaws and children soon gathered to cheer them. Most of the braves' faces, Hopkirk saw, were now daubed with paint. It was clear they were ready to do battle once more, to shed more blood, to finally wipe out the remainder of the hated pony soldiers in the canyon.

Hopkirk watched the demonstration's crescendo. Then he observed a boy run up to Diaglito's wick-

117

iup. He was leading his blood brother's sleek palomino horse. Hopkirk knew the beast was stolen from a rich Mexican rancher down Chihuahua some years ago.

Diaglito called the animal Wind Runner and Hopkirk knew there was a big reward waiting for the man who could return that magnificent creature to its rightful owner. There was just one snag to that: they needed to get past Diaglito first to do it.

With lithe grace the Apache war chief leapt on to the palomino's back. He waved his Winchester in the air. After making a wild circuit of the village leading his braves, he went off at a fast run toward the pine-clothed slope that would take him into mouth of the canyon, some three miles distant.

Yelling their courage cries, the braves closed in behind him. Despite all, it thrilled Hopkirk to watch this blood-stirring, primitive charge.

Hopkirk lowered the telescope he was using and returned it to Ryan. 'Guess it's time to take those horses, Pat.'

Ryan nodded, gravely. 'Can't come too soon for me, bucko.'

They did an Indian run along the shallow gully behind the bluff. It would take them quickly to the *tinaja* where the horses were being held. The rill was such good cover the possibility of being seen by the boys was minimal and the villagers' attention was still focused on Diaglito's wild departure from the plateau. Many villagers were running to the canyon top to view the spectacle of what they believed would be the slaughter of the rest of the patrol.

They took the boys completely by surprise. They put up some resistance – they wouldn't have been Apaches if they hadn't – but they were soon overwhelmed. The boys immediately recognized Hopkirk. Two spat at him and glared their hate. One shouted in Apache, 'Death to Hopkirk! Again he has betrayed us!'

Hopkirk said, quietly, 'Tie them up.'

Trooper Bosket Neil stared at him. 'We got to kill them, Captain. Nits make lice and they'll tell which way we gone.'

Hopkirk glared back at Neil. He said, 'Mister, there'll be no killing of children while I'm heading this party. Now, you being such a hard-ass, you get the job of covering their eyes and tying them up.' He gazed around him then. 'The rest of you, catch up your horses.' He pointed. 'Tackles over there by the looks of it.' Soon as he had run in he'd seen the patrol's bridles and saddles stashed under the trees, no doubt cached there waiting to be traded on in Mexico.

Hopkirk singled out Lieutenant James's frisky roan and caught it. The rest of the men soon captured their rides and saddled up. Neil was five minutes behind the rest and still clearly unhappy with the task he was given just now.

'Still say we should kill them,' he grumbled.

Again Hopkirk ignored him and climbed up and settled into the saddle. It was blessed relief. The climb in and out of the canyon on foot, he realized, had taken more out of him than he cared to admit. What was more, he felt as light as a feather and feverish. He waited for his head to clear.

Ryan said, 'You all right, Will?'

He nodded. 'All right.' The nausea was clearing. He looked around. 'Right, men, we drive the surplus horses ahead of us and, when we get them off the plateau, we scatter them. The last thing we want is Diaglito getting his hands on them.'

'After that?' Ryan said.

'We head for high ground and Fort Nathan.'

'Ain't you going through Snake Canyon?' Trooper Wyatt Lickmore said. 'It's the shortest way to the fort.'

Hopkirk wasn't averse to men asking questions or pointing out alternatives. He said, 'I agree, Trooper Lickmore, but that is exactly what Diaglito will expect us to do and that's why we're not going to do it.'

Lickmore pursed his lips. 'You're the boss . . . sir.'

Hopkirk eyed him. 'That it?'

'I guess so.'

Hopkirk nodded. 'OK, let's ride.'

The plan he offered sounded simple; nevertheless Hopkirk knew that every man there recognized it was far from being that. This was going to be a gut-churning ride all the way to Fort Nathan, accompanied by the very real prospect of never seeing another sunrise.

But anything was better than sitting on your ass in that canyon below waiting to die, Hopkirk decided – as they would have done had he not moved them out.

CHAPTER
FOURTEEN

Two hours after noon. The remains of the patrol were dismounted and resting. After eating hardtack and sipping water earlier, Hopkirk got them arranged along the top of the ridge that topped this immense, shelved canyon they had climbed out of an hour ago. They were watching Diaglito and his bucks making their way up the canyon side, completely unaware they were up here, waiting.

The several ledges that formed the canyon were timbered; pines on the upper slopes, sycamores, aspens, and cottonwoods on the lower slopes, willows in the bottom. A shallow stream flowed over the pebble-and-sand base.

While at the *tinaja* on the plateau where the cavalry horses were kept captive, they had filled their canteens. But though it was as hot as Hades right now on the top of this canyon and sweat was running freely from them, the troopers were drinking water sparingly. Most were old campaigners; all knew there was still a long way to go and finding other sources of water could prove difficult, despite Hopkirk's knowledge of the area.

Hopkirk trained Pat Ryan's telescope on Diaglito's band and brought them into focus. They were about a quarter of a mile below, easing their way up the shelves of yellow-red soil and rock.

Hopkirk counted twelve in all. Diaglito must have split his band; one half to cover the more direct route to Fort Nathan through Snake Pass, the other half to cover this route. Maybe the war chief figured he had acted similarly, to give at least half the survivors of the canyon attack a chance?

Pat Ryan was lying beside him. He said, 'What're your intentions, bucko?'

'It'll be another hour before they reach the top of the canyon,' Hopkirk said. 'It's a tough climb.'

'You haven't answered my question.'

Hopkirk gave his friend a searching glance. He said, 'I'm going to pin them down, get them nervous, hesitant and hope we win ourselves enough time to get to Wallace Canyon. After that we've got to play it by ear. My hope is John Dunstan will send out a relief column.'

'Where's the rest of Diaglito's party, you reckon?' Ryan said.

'Waiting in Snake Pass, figuring half of us may

head that way.'

'We'll be needing food,' Ryan said. 'Last of the hardtack was eaten just now.'

Hopkirk appraised his friend. 'You'd be surprised how long a man can go on just water, Pat, or even sucking on a pebble.'

'No I wouldn't,' Ryan said, 'because I've done both on occasion. But if I figure the way you're thinking, bucko, these men are not Apaches. Not only that, there are the horses to consider. I don't need to tell you we haven't got a chance in hell of getting out of here alive if they give out on us.'

Hopkirk said, 'There's water and grass where we're heading. If we get the chance we'll kill something to eat on the way.'

Trooper Wyatt Lickmore lying the other side of Hopkirk said, 'About Snake Canyon. . . .'

Hopkirk stared at the gaunt trooper. 'Go on.'

'I reckon Major Dunstan will be figuring we'll be coming in Snake Canyon way, being the shortest route to Fort Nathan, and not Wallace Canyon.'

'Go on.'

Lickmore spat a stream of plug juice over the rim rock and squinted sun-narrowed eyelids. 'How about me heading for Snake Canyon, meeting up with the major and steering him towards Wallace Canyon? Or, if he ain't, me riding on the Fort Nathan and breaking the news of the ambush?'

Hopkirk stared at the tall Texan. For damned

sure, there were no frills to this man and no deceit as far as he could make out, like deserting the column soon as he was out of sight.

He said, 'Sounds simple enough, but what experience have you got for that kind of work, Trooper? The Apaches aren't fools.'

Lickmore lifted a lean, darkly bristled chin. 'I was a Reb during the Insurrection. I rode with Jeb Stuart. Now, a man got to pick up a deal of cunning riding along with *that* man.'

Hopkirk was well acquainted with the renowned and fearless Rebel cavalryman Major General James Ewell Brown (J.E.B.) Stuart. He also knew Stuart and his men had caused endless trouble for the Federals behind their lines, and on the field of battle, before Stuart was killed at Yellow Tavern.

Hopkirk nodded. 'Well, that's some pedigree sure enough.' He tried to narrow his swollen eyelids. 'Out of curiosity, what made you join this man's army, Trooper? It couldn't have been easy for you.'

'Hunger, I guess,' Lickmore said, 'and I got to liking army ways. Fact is, I never did wholly get to know what I was fighting for with them Rebs. Jest went along for the ride, I guess.'

Hopkirk gave the man long appraisal: tall, lean, hard-eyed. He estimated Lickmore to be around forty. Going on that he could not have been much more than a boy when he joined the Rebel forces.

And clearly a life of soldiering had made him as tough as boot leather. Further, if Lickmore *could* get through it might make the difference. He looked at the man keenly.

'OK, trooper, soon as it's dark, move out.'

Lickmore nodded. 'Yes, sir.'

Hopkirk returned his attention to Diaglito and his bucks. They were traversing a long wide shelf now, heading for a steep gap in the red rock that would take them up to the next level. Before long, they would be spilling out over the canyon rim and he couldn't allow that.

He squinted against the burning afternoon sun. He estimated 150 yards separated them from the bucks. Just about right for putting his other plan into operation. He fondled the trapdoor Springfield rifle he had taken off the dead trooper in the canyon. Though it was not a repeater, the Springfield was formidable weapon in capable hands. He glanced at Ryan and attempted a grin. 'Reckon it's time to say hello, Pat,' he said.

Ryan frowned. 'Meaning?'

'I aim to pin them down for a spell.'

Enlightenment came to Ryan. 'Well, now.'

Hopkirk lined up his Springfield and set up the sights. He picked out Looking Glass. He was a deep-chested Mimbreño Apache who had married a White Mountain squaw and elected to live with Diaglito's tribe when the nuptials were complete.

He was known for his vile temper and his wife-beating tendencies. At this moment he was ruthlessly whipping his pony up the rocky slope. Hopkirk lined up the bead on him, steadied himself and squeezed off.

The rifle's boom sent echoes rampaging down the vast canyon. It shattered the silence and sent the birds into the air screaming warnings as they wheeled away up and down the canyon.

Instantly, Diaglito's band scattered like quail before a strong wind. Looking Glass flopped back, his yell coming clear on the hot rising air. He dropped off his pony and went bouncing down the steep, rocky side of the canyon until he went over the crest of an outcrop and into the tops of spruce fifty yards below. Then he plunged another 200 yards to the canyon floor.

Looking Glass, Hopkirk observed, was now a speck, lying on the streambed, runnels of water glinting in the hot sun as it flowed around his still body.

Calmly, Hopkirk lifted the trapdoor on the rifle and slid in another cartridge. He saw the rest of the bucks and Diaglito were now riding pell-mell along the shelf towards a big overhang, yipping their courage cries.

'Open fire, boys,' he said, 'two rounds!'

Rifles crackled into action. Another buck fell and white powder puffed off the red rock around the hard-riding bucks. Hopkirk lined up and fired once more, but this time he missed and he cursed.

When the braves finally scrambled into the cover, silence, like a door slamming to on Bedlam, settled over the canyon. But Hopkirk wasn't through. 'Give them a couple more, boys!'

Again lead exploded geysers of dust off the rocks and ricochets whined their deadly song. The bucks pressed back further into the shelter of the overhang. Hopkirk saw there was an almost sheer drop beyond the rock projection. Elation filled him. Glory of glories, Diaglito's band was effectively trapped. Not even a rattler could slide out of there with safety.

Wyatt Lickmore said, 'Sir, how about me hanging on here until dark; pepper them if they show their faces while you make it out of here.'

Hopkirk stared at him. 'Trooper, that's the best idea I've heard today. But don't take chances, we need you to get to Fort Nathan.'

Lickmore grinned and lovingly wiped dust off the sight of his Spencer carbine. 'Ol' Betsy will handle things here, sir, and I'll get to Fort Nathan; you can take bets on it. What's more, I'll get back.'

Hopkirk stared at the Texan with all seriousness. 'A lot is hanging on you pulling this off, Lickmore.'

'I know that, sir.'

Hopkirk nodded. He looked along the rest of the men lying on the canyon's lip. 'OK, crawl back and mount up, men.'

Five minutes later they were riding out and Lickmore was powdering the rock behind which the Apaches waited.

CHAPTER FIFTEEN

Coming on sundown the remnants of the patrol entered grama grass meadows. The horses were tethered on long ropes attached to the picket line close to the sycamores that were growing near the *tinaja* that was also there. Before long the animals were cropping the nutritious grass.

Martin Lish, riding point, had earlier killed a white tail buck. Hopkirk was not unduly concerned about the noise the rifle made. The direction from where the echoes came would be confusing in this maze of canyons and mesas ... even for the Apaches. In any case, if Diaglito did manage to pinpoint the noise and put two and two together, the remnants of the patrol would be long gone by the time his braves got on their trail once more because occasionally, he heard the faint crash of a rifle. No doubt about it, Lickmore was still pinning down those Apaches.

A near smokeless fire was started under an overhang, to disperse what smoke there was and the buck was skinned, jointed and meat required for immediate use was seared in the flames.

As soon as the scorching was done the fire was stamped out and the leftover meat was laid aside for packing later. Flies were particularly a menace. They were thick in the air and displaying their voracious appetite for blood and flesh. It was a constant battle to keep them at bay.

Come nightfall, the faint, intermittent booms of Lickmore's now familiar rifle ceased. Eating was suspended and all eyes turned in the direction of the canyon, blood and juices running down bristly chins ignored.

Hopkirk blinked into the evening gloom. A hell of a lot was riding on Lickmore now. He wiped his chin and looked around at the troopers.

'Right, men, playtime's over; fill your canteens and spares, pack what's left of the meat and get mounted.' As he spoke, the moon rose huge and silver and luminous above the purple-dark bulks to the east.

The orders given, they were quickly carried out. Horses and the now mounted men looked fresher for the food and rest. Hopkirk mounted, gritting his teeth against the pain it caused and said, 'OK, men, let's get out of here.'

He led them off the top of the undulating meadows and down the long, steep boulder-strewn north-facing slope. Reaching bottom he pushed on at a steady canter. Two miles up the valley Hopkirk knew there was yet another canyon to deal with and this one was a real humdinger.

Soon long vicious thorns were tearing at horse and man and ripping away at already tattered uniforms. Horses grunted, nickered and men cursed as flesh was torn. After an hour's tortuous travel they entered into a long rocky defile leaving the thorn scrub behind.

Hopkirk knew this narrow ravine was made for ambush, but he decided Diaglito could not have reached this area yet. That being the case, he considered it would be safe to travel through it without much caution. However, having come to that conclusion he knew a man could never be quite certain of anything where Apaches were concerned. But all seemed quiet and he walked his horse forward with reasonable confidence.

After a silence of more than an hour and a half Pat Ryan said, 'Will, I reckon with a little strategy we could cause some real mischief in this place. It's built for ambush. Seems a pity to waste it.'

Always open to suggestions, Hopkirk stared at the sergeant through the strong moon glow. 'Go on.'

'We hide in the rocks and wait,' went on Ryan. 'There's enough light to see by and Diaglito won't be expecting us to try for him right now; he'll be thinking we'll have one thought in our heads . . .

132

making a run for Fort Nathan.'

Hopkirk studied the stocky Irishman for some moments while he mulled over the proposition then he said, 'It won't work, Pat. Apaches don't fight at night unless the odds are high in their favour. First shot we fire they'll melt into the rocks and be gone. But come dawn, because we've shown our hand, they will be down on us like a ton of bricks.'

But it was clear Ryan wasn't through yet. 'In that case we pick big targets, shoot their horses from under them; put them afoot. Our first volley should get enough to slow them down considerable.'

Hopkirk gave out with a patient sigh. 'Pat, I thought you knew the Apache better than that. Afoot or in the saddle he is formidable and he'll come on.'

Ryan said, 'Yeah, but even Apaches get tired, Will, and if the plan works it'll give us enough breathing space to get us through to Fort Nathan.'

'And if it doesn't?'

'Diaglito's only got twelve braves; we'll match him, even better him. Maybe that is what we should do.'

Hopkirk said, 'He's got others watching Snake Canyon, Pat, and right now my bet is they'll be waiting on the trail Lickmore's riding. That's why I was reluctant to let him try what he proposed. However, when he mentioned riding with Jeb

Stuart it put a different complexion on the matter. With that kind of experience I figure he'll have a more than an even chance of getting through. But as soon as we show our hand here Diaglito will call in those men watching Snake Canyon. He won't be bothered about Lickmore getting through once he gets to know where the rest of the patrol are. And killing the rest of the patrol will be big medicine for him and maybe it will incite others to join him, which they haven't done up to now. One way or another, Pat, once Diaglito knows where we are, he'll encircle us and finish us off before the relief column can get anywhere near us – that's always counting on Lickmore getting through. Then he'll be long gone, raiding ranches and settlements before heading for Mexico to rest on his laurels.'

'I still think it's worth a try,' Ryan said stubbornly.

'Not right now it isn't. Let's get to the high ground.'

As they came out of the ravine, Wallace Canyon opened up before them. Hopkirk led them up the grassy channels flanked by house-size boulders toward the top of the west ridge.

As he rode he pondered further on Ryan's plan and found some sympathy for it. But it was too late now. In any case, he figured he was well ahead of Diaglito so it didn't really matter.

By the time they reached the top of the canyon

the horses were blowing hard. Hopkirk turned to the column behind him. 'OK. Take two hours, men; give the horses a rest and try to get some sleep. We could have a big day ahead of us tomorrow.'

Looks of surprise greeted him but the troopers climbed down. Soon the horses were picketed and they were sleeping.

Lying nearby in his blanket, Ryan said, 'Why the stop? You were all for putting distance between them Apaches and us a while ago.'

Hopkirk tried to get his scarred body comfortable, but he could not help grunting at the pain. After moments he said, 'Pat, men and horses have been driven hard these past few days. A little rest and sleep will do them good. For what lies ahead we need fit horses and fit men. Soon all our lives may well depend on that. And we've got the high ground. Come dawn we will be able to see for miles and can plan our strategy. I figure a fast run in to Fort Nathan is now possible.'

Ryan said, 'I sure hope to God you're right.'

The burly sergeant rolled over on to his right side and pulled up his blanket. Soon he was snoring heavily.

Meanwhile, Hopkirk listened to the night. His body was a mass of pain and the waves of nausea he was experiencing caused him to wonder if he ordered this halt because he couldn't handle the constant agony of jolting about in the saddle, or whether it was a sensible strategy.

No, dammit, he thought fiercely, he was right to call a halt.

CHAPTER SIXTEEN

Dawn was signalling its imminent arrival by lighting the eastern horizon with salmon-pink light. Soon the dark blue of the sky to the west retreated and began to pale to lilac.

Hopkirk woke up alert and ready for action, surprised he had slept. As he moved, his hurts once more sent pain rampaging through him, but the wounds were not so bad as they were and he began to think he might pull through this without serious infection. The itching he was undergoing, as well as the soreness, he decided, was also a good sign healing was in progress.

He saw Bosket Neil was already out of his blanket, standing yawning and stretching in the orange light of the chill dawn. The rest of the troopers were still lying prone, rubbing sleep out of their eyes. Hopkirk assumed Pat Ryan must have woken them moments ago. The Irishman, he observed, was now up at the picket line checking on the condition of the horses.

The crash of the shot rang stark and sudden on the pristine morning. It came from the opposite side of the canyon and Neil let out a yell and threw up his arms and staggered back. Hopkirk saw a black hole was stamped into the centre of his forehead and a sickening spray of blood and brains was coming out of the back of his skull and splattering down on Trooper Roger Coots, who was sitting on his blanket at the back of him.

Coots yelped as the matter sprayed on to his tunic and unshaven face. Still reeling back Neil fell over him and on to the grass to lie still. Coots sprang up, horror on his face.

'Get down, you damned fool!' Hopkirk said.

Coots was already realizing his mistake and dropped to the ground. Now he looked with anxious eyes to the opposite rim of the canyon while fumbling for his Remington conversion six-shooter under the bow of his saddle. As he brought the gun up two more shots whacked into the bright morning from the other side of the canyon.

Hopkirk shouted, 'Get to your rifles, men, and take cover!'

Coots cut loose with his Remington, but at this range Hopkirk knew there was slim hope the trooper was going to hit anything but he appreciated Coots's effort would have nuisance value.

He scrambled behind a boulder, his Springfield already in hand. With alert eyes he searched the opposite rim rock ... three White Mountain Apaches atop wiry ponies. They were whooping and waving rifles, challenging them. Hopkirk knew them all: Notsin, Askinay, Ukleni – all part of Diaglito's band. He could only guess how they got there, maybe sheer happenstance.

He brought his rifle to his shoulder. Ideally, he should take out all three before they could get word back to Diaglito, but he knew there wasn't even a remote chance of him doing that so he picked out Askinay. He knew the man to be a good fighter with knife and rifle and an excellent tracker. He was the most useful man of the three to Diaglito.

Taking aim Hopkirk squeezed off.

Askinay's yell came clear and clean across the gap between them, but he managed to stay in his blanket saddle.

Hopkirk was opening the smoking trapdoor on his rifle and sliding in another load when the braves whooped and turned their ponies and galloped off down the gentle wooded slope Hopkirk knew from previous acquaintance was at the back of the canyon's rim.

A staccato volley from the now fully alert troopers followed them until they sank out of sight, then the firing stopped.

Pat Ryan came running in from the horses.

'Thought we were free of the red devils.'

'So did I,' Hopkirk said bitterly.

Ryan said, 'You got any ideas?'

Hopkirk was already racking his brains. 'I reckon this could be nothing but chance. I think they were men on a hunting trip. No paint, but they'll soon be getting back to Diaglito now.' He pointed a long finger. 'There's a long narrow valley yonder. It'll take us into the badlands. The boys and horses are well rested, so we should be able to build up a lead, enough to give us a chance of getting to Fort Nathan or to meet the relief column heading our way, banking on Trooper Lickmore getting through that is – if he gets through.'

'*If* is the operative word,' Ryan said.

Hopkirk nodded. 'Yes. Get the men saddled up, Pat, and let's get out of here.'

Equipment gathered, horses saddled and mounted, Hopkirk led the men down through the pines and aspens. Golden early morning sunlight speared dark lines through the branches of the trees on to the carpet of brown pine needles and the other leaves they were riding over.

Reaching the bottom, Hopkirk led the men up the narrow valley at a canter. He found himself cautiously optimistic. As far as he could make out there wasn't an Apache in sight nor was there likely to be . . . yet.

He soon found he was living in a fool's paradise.

Less than half an hour on they heard the drums beating and saw the smoke rise. Twenty minutes later Hopkirk detected faint whoops coming from behind.

An icy band of fear grabbed at his stomach. He swung round in the saddle. He saw the Apaches were filtering out of the trees a good half-mile to his rear. Oddly, they were whipping a horse and rider ahead of them. The horse's squeals came clear to them on the cool morning air, due, no doubt, to the cruel treatment. Then the beast began galloping toward them up the valley.

It was a big horse, a cavalry horse. The rider on its back was dressed in federal blue. However, Hopkirk noticed the man's carriage in the saddle was strange. He sat too stiff, too erect.

He didn't look right at all.

The horse's squealing also aroused the horses of the patrol. They began whistling a reply to the whipped animal. The beast began coming towards them. Soon it was amongst them and Trooper Lish caught the trailing rein.

It was shivering, its eyes rolling wild. Hopkirk's heart sank like a stone when he saw it was Trooper Lickmore on its back, dead as he ever would be. But that was only the start of it. Hopkirk noticed Lickmore's legs were fastened tightly to the horse's barrel and that his torso was tied to a stout willow frame, which was what was holding him in that strange, upright position. But much worse followed.

Through the trooper's open tunic Hopkirk saw a horror of striped flesh; not enough to kill him mind – unless his heart gave out – just enough to cause him excruciating pain. Hopkirk eased his mount forward. Lickmore's head was slumped down and resting on his chest. His campaign hat, which was jammed on his head, was pulled down to cover his eyes and half his face.

Half knowing what to expect, Hopkirk leaned forward and carefully removed the hat. The top of Lickmore's skull was roasted, enough to crack it apart to reveal charred brains. But that was not the end of it, he knew. Hopkirk leaned over and lifted Lickmore's slow-baked head. The trooper's eye sockets were empty black holes staring back at him.

Lish said, 'Oh, Jesus,' and dropped the rein on Lickmore's horse and leaned over and threw up his last meal into the grass.

Grim-faced, Hopkirk stared north, up the valley. He wasn't surprised to see a larger group of Apaches coming towards them out of the conifers and aspens clothing the valley sides up there.

They were effectively boxed in and he thought: neat job, my brother. But we're not through yet.

He looked about him. One thing, he knew this valley. He knew there was a boulder-clustered rise of ground a quarter of a mile along the top of the ridge that formed part of the western slope to their left. He knew it was a natural fortress. He turned to the troopers, who were anxiously eyeing him as well as the approaching braves and said, 'OK, boys, follow me.'

He grabbed the rein on Lickmore's horse and then urged his frisky mount up the west slope. Almost immediately shrill whoops came from the two groups of braves ahead and behind and they put their ponies into a flat out run. Hopkirk set his chin into a grim line.

The chase was really on now.

CHAPTER SEVENTEEN

At the top of the valley, they burst out of the trees on to a flat rock plateau spotted with scrub. Hopkirk swung his mount west while all the time allowing his eyes to search the terrain around him, hoping his memory still held good.

There it was, the natural fortification on a rise of ground some half a mile on and 100 or so yards back from the valley's ridge.

He turned his horse toward it while tugging the rein on the beast supporting Trooper Lickmore's carcass. Within seconds he piled into the shallow hollow that formed the natural fortification on the mound of ground and dismounted. The remnants of the patrol were close behind, dismounting on the run.

Rifles in hand, Colts in regulation belt holsters

and ammunition pouches full, the men scrambled towards the protection of the rocks edging the small basin while Coots picketed the horses in the middle of the hollow.

They were vulnerable, Hopkirk knew, but there was little that could be done about that now. Horse and man would have to take his chance.

Hopkirk cut Lickmore's body free from his horse and laid his body on the ground.

That done, with Coots, he joined the men at the ramparts.

They were hardly in place when the first of the braves came running or galloping out of the trees and across the flat scrub ground toward them. They were whooping like demons.

The men looked anxiously at Hopkirk.

'Wait for my order, boys,' he called, 'then give them two volleys. Independent fire after that, if there is anything to hit.'

He knew they were seasoned troopers and hoped they would hold until the right time and conserve their lead when there were no targets to hit.

The Apaches were now nearly thirty yards away, formed up in a full-blooded charge.

They were already pumping lead and firing arrows, which were humming and hissing all around, too close for comfort.

Hopkirk saw Diaglito was at their head. He made a magnificent figure as he charged towards this natural fortification.

Hopkirk held the order to fire until the last moment then yelled,

'Now, boys!'

The first volley rang out and three Apache blanket saddles emptied. Two running braves staggered, their faces screwed up in pain as they dropped.

The group split pronto, taking their dead with them, as Hopkirk expected them to do. But he was satisfied. Diaglito's bunch was too thin on the ground to lose that many men in one charge and not get cautious. In a strange way he was oddly relieved to see Diaglito was not amongst those fallen.

The second volley from the troopers followed the Apaches as they scattered into the trees. Another buck fell and was scooped up by following braves before the whole lot of them melted into cover.

The firing ceased abruptly and a long silence fell over the area like a brooding cloud. It lasted long enough for the birds to start singing again. And all the time the heat of the morning grew as the sun rose. Handkerchiefs were pulled out to mop brows and necks. The cursing amongst the troopers was heart-felt. Hopkirk could only grit his teeth as the salt in sweat bit into his wounds.

But . . . what the hell was Diaglito waiting for?

Another hour dragged by, then Trooper Coots fired his Springfield rifle startling the men into abrupt alertness. Coots was reloading his rifle when Ryan said,

'You see something, Coots?'

'Thought I did.'

Hpkirk said, 'Dammit, that's what they want us to do, shoot at shadows. Make sure you have a target, Trooper.'

Coots said, 'I saw something, dammit!'

A volley of shots came from the trees and soil and pebbles splintered the ground atop this natural fortification. But some of the lead, Hopkirk noticed, came *down* into the hollow. One piece of lead tore a chunk out of Trooper Harvey Kitts's right boot heel.

'They're in the trees,' he yelled. Hopkirk called, 'Fire if you see a target.'

Drowning his words a shot rang out and an agonized scream followed. A body crashed through branches before hitting the rocky ground with a bony crunch. Coots whooped his delight. 'I git one this time, by God!'

Ryan fired. Another Indian fell out of the trees like a floppy rag doll bouncing off branches before hitting the ground.

Now Hopkirk heard Diaglito talking, urgently. Soon there were glimpses of braves shinning down the hidden side of trunks.

Hopkirk decided his men showed remarkable restraint not firing at brief glimpses of bodies as they descended. And it was becoming increasingly obvious they were hard, tough men with wide experience of fighting these desert killers. For sure, with this bunch, there was a real chance of getting out of this alive.

Half an hour of gut-churning tension followed as the heat got more intense. Hopkirk became concerned. Too much water was being drunk. He was about to tell the men to go easy when firing from the rear and a yell of pain stopped his warning. Trooper Puckas and Coots were doing the watching and shooting back there.

He said, 'They got round the back of us?'

Puckas cleared his throat. 'Thought I saw something.'

'Keep your eyes peeled,' Hopkirk said. He turned to Lish, lying close by. 'Get over there and help them.'

Lish crawled away.

After an hour of sniping the Apaches began to pick off the horses. Hopkirk wondered why it had taken them so long to get round to that, but good horses were hard to come by and prime cavalry horses always made a good price in Mexico. And Apaches, not having much use for money, usually traded horses for coffee, clothes and sometimes mules, favourite meat of theirs. Rifles and ammunition were also traded, the dealers often unscrupulous white men out to make a buck.

The Apaches downed three of the scrawniest animals. Hopkirk dispatched the one that didn't die immediately and was threshing about kicking Lickmore's carcass to ribbons with iron-shod hoofs. The rest shied away.

The morning went quiet once more. Then Diaglito came to the edge off the trees, a white flag in his hand, and walked to a mark halfway between the lines. Hopkirk's blood froze when he saw Sonseray was struggling in his grasp. There were signs of a beating on her face. The rattle of rifles cocking sounded all around him and put him even more on edge.

'Hold your fire, men,' he said. 'That is my wife.'

Seven hard stares fastened on to him and Trooper Lish said, 'The hell it is. So, the God damned rumours are true.'

'Button it, Lish.' Ryan said.

Ignoring Lish, Hopkirk stood up and stepped out of the perimeter and walked towards Diaglito. When he got up close he said, in Apache, 'It is not like the great war chief of the White Mountain Apache to hide behind a woman.'

Diaglito said gravely, 'I am going to give you a chance, my brother. Don't ask me why I should do this. It cannot give you an answer.'

'Perhaps Diaglito cannot kill his daughter,' Hopkirk said.

Diaglito smiled, faintly. 'How little you know of

us, my brother,' he said. 'She has broken the laws of our people. The penalty for that is death. But if you are prepared to fight for her and win, you and she could go free.'

Hopkirk narrowed his eyelids, darted his eyes across the faces of the bucks standing on the edge of the trees. 'Is this is a trick?'

'You know I would not cheat my brother.'

There was still suspicion in Hopkirk. 'Do the people behind you see it that way?'

Diaglito shook his head. 'No, they want the blood of Sonseray, but I persuaded them to let you fight for her and they have agreed because they know you and honour you because of your help in times past, even though they wanted to kill you at the stake. If I die they will ride away and Sonseray will come to you.'

More suspicion grew in Hopkirk. 'I still find this strange behaviour for the Apache.'

Diaglito's fierce, dark face grew long. 'The truth is, *mi hermano*, my people are tired. Too many have died and we grow fewer by the day. They do not want to make war any more.' Diaglito paused and shrugged, a little sadly. 'I thought other tribes would join me when I made my war because of the injustice meted out to them over long years, but this did not happen. They all say the white men are too strong for them now.'

'I told you this,' Hopkirk said.

'You did.'

Hopkirk said, 'What happens if it is I who dies?'

'Sonseray will be killed and all of you will die here and I will lead my people into Mexico.'

Hopkirk waved a hand to the rear and said, 'These men will have something to say about that, *mi hermano*. And Bear Coat Miles will follow you and kill you, or send you to Florida if he captures you.'

'This is the risk we take,' Diaglito said. He switched to English, his stare intense. 'Take this chance, my brother; I fought hard to get it for you.'

Hopkirk set his strong jaw. From behind Ryan hissed, 'What the hell is going on, bucko?'

Hopkirk told him of Diaglito's offer.

Ryan said, 'Forget it, Will. You're not fit to fight; he'll tear you apart. Tell him to go to hell; we'll take our chances.'

'I can't do that. Sonseray would die, and my unborn child—'

'She's pregnant?' Ryan said.

'Yes.'

'Those bastards won't keep their promise,' Ryan said.

'I think they will,' Hopkirk said.

He turned to Diaglito. 'What weapon do you choose, my brother?'

'The knife is always good; there is skill in it.'

Hopkirk nodded, soberly. 'So be it.'

151

'So be it.'

And the killing ritual began in accordance with the law of the Apache.

CHAPTER EIGHTEEN

Hopkirk stripped off his tunic to reveal his slashed chest. A look told him the wounds seemed to be healing well.

Ryan's whiskey was doing a good job.

He wiped his sweaty right hand down his rough trousers and palmed his big Bowie knife and stood waiting.

Diaglito looked at his scarred body and admiration lit up his dark eyes. He nodded. 'I see my brother is truly a warrior, as I always knew. The torture has not quenched your courage.'

Hopkirk did not reply, just concentrated as he watched a circle being drawn into the thin, dusty soil. Lance men were posted at intervals around, ready to encourage an erring combatant back into the circle of death should he stray or be forced over the crudely drawn line.

Though he was not young any more Diaglito

stripped off his deerskin tunic to reveal a finely muscled bronze torso. Scars showed, badges of many encounters against white and red man.

Pesh-chidin, the medicine man of Diaglito's tribe came forward. He took Diaglito's knife and Hopkirk's. He offered the two blades to the four corners of the world and muttered guttural words, blessing the glinting steel.

When the ceremony was over Pesh-chidin stared at Hopkirk.

'You understand the rules, Hopkirk?'

'Yes.'

Pesh-chidin nodded gravely and said,

'Then may life ebb cleanly.'

Diaglito said, 'As it is written.'

'As it is written,' Hopkirk said.

As was the custom the White Mountain war chief took the knives and tossed the blades to the ground, one each side of the circle, roughly twenty yards apart.

Hopkirk did not hesitate. He ran for his blade and took it up, the haft feeling good and familiar in his hand. He swung round to see Diaglito already coming towards him, his finely chiselled features tense and ultra alert, his blade flashing in his hand. Evading Diaglito's first pass Hopkirk's back slash missed the war chief's kidneys by inches. Dust rose.

After that first pass Hopkirk circled warily. Diaglito came forward swiftly, slashing with his knife in a criss-cross fashion. Hopkirk evaded the sweeps, but not by much. He moved closer switching his blade to his left hand. It was the border shift. Hopkirk believed it to be developed by the early Texans. It was a Lone Star man who had taught him the move, anyway.

Diaglito narrowed his eyelids and began circling, studying the move. Hopkirk danced ever nearer, taking advantage of Diaglito's momentary uncertainty and stabbing and sweeping for the chest and heart. His probing paid off. He felt slight connection and Diaglito grimaced and, to evade his sweeps, dropped to the ground, rolled and came up crouched and ready.

Blood was running from the shallow gash across his ribs.

Diaglito came forward quickly, veered at the last moment and Hopkirk found he was being upended by a sweeping kick. And as he fell he felt keen steel slice across his back.

He gasped at the sudden pain, rolled aside, grabbing Diaglito's ankle as he went. He twisted the foot and the war chief lost balance and toppled, sprawling on to the dust and pebbles.

Hopkirk was up in an instant. Moving rapidly he stamped down on Diaglito's wrist, pinning his knife hand to the ground. Then he bent and pressed his own knife against Diaglito's exposed throat, while his other hand swiped away the blade in Diaglito's hand, forced open by the pressure of the boot on his wrist.

Hopkirk looked into Diaglito's eyes; they were the colour of obsidian as they stared up at him.

The war chief said, 'Strike cleanly, my brother, let there be no hate between us.'

Indecision racked Hopkirk. Yells to kill were coming from the troopers behind him, but the braves were silent. Dammit, he thought, he *should* kill Diaglito, there was too much at stake, but he couldn't. He stood there, knife poised over Diaglito's throat.

Then he became aware that Sonseray was pleading,

'Do not kill him, my husband!'

It was Trooper Lish's yell that broke the gut-searing stalemate. His call was jubilant.

'By God, it's Major Dunstan; I'll bet my boots on it.'

Hopkirk turned to see Lish was pointing down into the valley. Then the trooper waved his rifle in the air and fired off two shots.

Moments later the brassy notes of a cavalry bugle came from the valley below.

Hopkirk let go of Diaglito and stepped away to stare down into the valley over the tops of the trees.

He saw a column of about fifty troopers turning their horses to come up through the trees towards them.

The Apaches saw the troopers, too. They began running for their horses yelling and whooping warnings. One turned as he was passing Sonseray and lifted his blade to strike. Hopkirk threw his Bowie. The broad blade buried itself deeply between the brave's shoulder blades.

The warrior yelped and staggered and tried to reach and grab the haft before dropping to the ground to die, blood spurting out of his mouth.

Diaglito, Hopkirk now saw, was on his feet. He was picking up his knife and running for his palomino.

Rifles began to crack from the defences behind Hopkirk. Two braves fell. One of them was Diaglito.

The sight of his brother falling galvanized Hopkirk. Forgetting the situation he was in he ran to the fallen chief and knelt beside him. Diaglito was already chanting his death song – deep, throbbing notes that echoed across the red-rock canyons of his homeland. Hopkirk gripped him by the shoulder.

'Lie still, my brother,' he said. 'Perhaps we can save you.'

Diaglito stopped chanting. Something akin to love seemed to light up his otherwise pain-filled eyes. He smiled. 'If only all men could find each other as we have done, *mi hermano*, what a wonderful place our land would be.' With that he fell back and sighed, closed his eyes and died.

It was then Sonseray came into Hopkirk's arms and pressed against him and stood there, saying nothing, just holding him and staring at Diaglito.

Eventually, Hopkirk became aware that blood was running down his back from the wound Diaglito inflicted. He also realized some of his other wounds were seeping blood, however, he clung to Sonseray, wanting her, feeling the warmth of her body pressed against his, the love in her seeping into him and he reciprocating it. It negated all his other worries.

They stood together even though fifty blue-coated men now broke out of the trees and started after the fleeing braves.

Major John Dunstan was at their head. When Dunstan saw him he reined in his horse and came towards him, ordering Lieutenant Phillip Dryden to continue the chase after the White Mountain Apaches who were streaming away through the pines towards the mountains and canyons.

Dunstan leaned over in the saddle on his sweating dun horse and said, 'You look as though you've been in the wars, Will.'

Hopkirk said, 'You could say that. But it ends here, John. I resign my commission, as of now.'

Dunstan frowned. 'I don't follow.'

Hopkirk compressed his swollen lips. 'I have other responsibilities, John. I should have met them first off, but I didn't.'

Dunstan continued to frown. 'I still don't understand.'

'You don't need to,' Hopkirk said.

Hopkirk pulled Sonseray closer to him, and, arm around her, he walked towards his horse. At that moment Diaglito's shivering palomino walked up to them to stand by Diaglito's still body.

Hopkirk reached for the rein leading from the rawhide hackamore about the palomino's head. Then he bent and almost reverently picked up Diaglito's body and placed it on the palomino's back, face down. After that he found rope and fastened the body to it.

Mounting his own horse, he pulled Sonseray up behind him.

John Dunstan was still frowning at him. 'What is this, Will? Don't you even want to be in on the kill?' He eyed the scout's knife-scarred body. 'Looks to me as though you've earned the right.'

'I've had enough of killing, John. I'm ending it right here.'

Dustan looked at him keenly before he said, 'Well, I know enough about you not to argue when you are in this mood. Maybe when you're—'

Hopkirk said, 'No maybes, John. This is for keeps.'

With that he kneed his horse into a walk. He took up the rawhide lead rope on Diaglito's palomino and headed for the cabin in the canyon.

He would bury Diaglito in the Apache way, as a brother should. After that he would ... he felt Sonseray's arms tighten around his waist. He heard her sigh happily as she pressed her beautiful body against his scarred torso. He decided, right at this moment, 'then' was another day and could wait just a little while longer. For right now there were more important things to consider.

1
- 8

2 ?
1 6

7

2

DONCASTER LIBRARY

30122 03138068 2